Also by L. Divine

THE FIGHT

SECOND CHANCE

JAYD'S LEGACY

FRENEMIES

LADY J

COURTIN' JAYD

HUSTLIN'

KEEP IT MOVIN'

HOLIDAZE

CULTURE CLASH

COLD AS ICE

Published by Kensington Publishing Corporation

Drama High, Vol. 12

PUSHIN'

L. Divine

WITHDRAWN

KENSINGTON PUBLISHING CORP.
www.kensingtonbooks.com

DAFINA BOOKS are published by

Kensington Publishing Corp.
119 West 40th Street
New York, NY 10018

All Kensington titles, imprints, and distributed lines are available at special quantity discounts for bulk purchases for sales promotion, premiums, fund-raising, educational, or institutional use.

Special book excerpts or customized printings can also be created to fit specific needs. For details, write or phone the office of the Kensington Special Sales Manager: Kensington Publishing Corp., 119 West 40th Street, New York, NY 10018. Attn. Special Sales Department. Phone: 1-800-221-2647.

Dafina and the Dafina logo Reg. U.S. Pat. & TM Off.

ISBN-13: 978-0-7582-3115-4
ISBN-10: 0-7582-3115-6

First Kensington Trade Paperback Printing: October 2010

10 9 8 7 6 5 4 3

Printed in the United States of America

This book is dedicated . . .

To Julie Ingle, a true mama friend. I don't know what I would have done without such a good friend and neighbor those first few months of new motherhood. Blessings to you and your family always.

And to teenage mothers taking care of their business: No matter how early in your life motherhood may come, your strength, patience, and prevailing energy is what ushers in a new generation. Don't forget you deserve to grow up, too.

ACKNOWLEDGMENTS

"It takes courage to grow up and turn out to be who you really are."

—E. E. CUMMINGS

To the people who have excelled personally and professionally because of Drama High: Keep on pushing, because I know I will. To my publisher, Dafina/Kensington: twelve books down and we are still moving forward. Thank you always for your support. And finally, to my readers: As I have said before, as long as you keep reading, I'll keep writing. Thank you very much for your loyalty always. Keep flowing, keep hustling, keep working, keep praying, keep moving, keep striving, and keep pushing.

THE CREW

Jayd

A sassy seventeen-year-old from Compton, California, who comes from a long line of Louisiana conjure women. She is the only one in her lineage born with brown eyes and a caul. Her grandmother appropriately named her "Jayd," which is also the name her grandmother took on in her days as a voodoo queen in New Orleans. Jayd now lives in her mother's apartment in Inglewood. She visits her grandmother on the weekends in Compton, her former home. Jayd is in all AP classes. She has a tense relationship with her father, whom she sees occasionally, and has never-ending drama in her life, whether at school or home.

Mama/Lynn Mae

When Jayd gets in over her head, her grandmother, Mama, is always there to help her. A full-time conjure woman with magical green eyes and a long list of both clients and haters, Mama also serves as Jayd's teacher, confidante, and protector.

Mom/Lynn Marie

At thirty-something years old, Lynn Marie would never be mistaken for a mother of a teenager. Jayd's mom is definitely all that and with her green eyes, she keeps the men guessing. Able to talk to Jayd telepathically, Lynn Marie is always there when Jayd needs her.

Netta

The owner of Netta's Never Nappy Beauty Shop, Netta is Mama's best friend, business partner, and godsister in their religion. She also serves as a godmother to Jayd, who works part-time at Netta's Shop.

Esmeralda

Mama's nemesis and Jayd's nightmare, this next-door neighbor is anything but friendly. She relocated to Compton from Louisiana around the same time Mama did and has been a thorn in Mama's side ever since. She continuously causes trouble for Mama and Jayd. Esmeralda's cold blue eyes have powers of their own, although not nearly as powerful as Mama's.

Rah

Rah is Jayd's first love from junior high school, who has come back into her life when a mutual friend, Nigel, transfers from Rah's high school (Westingle) to South Bay. He knows everything about her and is her spiritual confidant. Rah lives in Los Angeles but grew up with his grandparents in Compton like Jayd. He loves Jayd fiercely but has a baby-mama who refuses to go away. Rah is a hustler by necessity and a music producer by talent. He takes care of his younger brother, Kamal, and holds the house down while his dad is locked up and his mother strips at a local club.

Misty

The word "frenemies" was coined for this former best friend of Jayd's. Misty has made it her mission to sabotage Jayd any way she can. Living around the corner from Jayd, she has the unique advantage of being an original hater from the neighborhood and at school.

KJ

He's the most popular basketball player on campus, Jayd's ex-boyfriend, and Misty's current boyfriend. Ever since he and Jayd broke up, he's made it his personal mission to persecute her.

Nellie

One of Jayd's best friends, Nellie is the prissy princess of the crew. She is also dating Chance, even though it's Nigel she's really feeling. Nellie made history at South Bay by becoming the first black Homecoming princess and has let the crown go to her head.

Mickey

The gangster girl of Jayd's small crew, she and Nellie are best friends but often at odds with each other, mostly because Nellie secretly wishes she could be more like Mickey. A true hood girl, she loves being from Compton, and her ex-man with no name is a true gangster. Mickey and Nigel have quickly become South Bay High's newest couple.

Jeremy

A first for Jayd, Jeremy is her white on again/off again boyfriend who also happens to be the most popular cat at South Bay. Rich, tall, and extremely handsome, Jeremy's witty personality and good conversation keep Jayd on her toes and give Rah a run for his money—literally.

Mickey's Man

Never using his name, Mickey's original boyfriend is a troublemaker and always hot on Mickey's trail. Always in and out of jail, Mickey's man is notorious in her hood for being a coldhearted gangster, and loves to be in control. He also has a thing for Jayd, but Jayd can't stand to be anywhere near him.

Nigel

The new quarterback on the block, Nigel is a friend of Jayd's from junior high and also Rah's best friend, making Jayd's world even smaller at South Bay High. Nigel is the star football player and dumped his ex-girlfriend at Westingle (Tasha) to be with his new baby-mama-to-be, Mickey. Jayd is caught up in the mix as a friend to them both, but her loyalty lies with Nigel because she's known him longer and he's always had her back.

Chance

The rich, white hip-hop kid of the crew, Chance is Jayd's drama homie and Nellie's boyfriend, if you let him tell it. He used to have a crush on Jayd and now has turned his attention to Nellie for the time being. Chance's dreams of being black come true when he discovers he was adopted. His biological mother is half black, and his birth name is Chase.

Bryan

The youngest of Mama's children and Jayd's favorite uncle, Bryan is a dj by night and works at the local grocery store during the day. He's also an acquaintance of both Rah and KJ from playing ball around the hood. Bryan often gives Jayd helpful advice about her problems with boys and hating girls alike. Out of all of Jayd's uncles, Bryan gives her grandparents the least amount of trouble.

Jay

Jay is more like an older brother to Jayd than her cousin. He lives with Mama, but his mother (Mama's youngest daughter, Anne) left him when he was a baby and never returned. He doesn't know his father and attends Compton High. He and Jayd often cook together and help Mama around the house.

Prologue

Ever since I left Rah's house Friday evening he's been blowing my cell up and I just don't have the energy to deal with his bull. Mama and I have been cooking all afternoon, providing me with the perfect distraction. After eating a slamming dinner of chicken, rice, greens, and cornbread, a sistah is stuffed. All I really want to do is pass out on my mom's couch and watch television for the rest of the night, but I doubt Mama's letting me go anytime soon. Since moving out of Mama's house a few weeks ago to live at my mom's apartment, Mama's made it her personal mission to keep me here as long as she possibly can on my now regular Sunday visits. And as long as I can get a good meal out of it I won't protest too much, even if the itis is setting in.

"Jayd, hand me that white fabric on the table, please," Mama says from where she's seated on the floor across from the kitchen table. I stack the last of the clean dishes on the rack, dry my hands off on one of the yellow kitchen towels hanging from the cabinet above the sink, and hand her the stack of folded cloth.

"Thank you," Mama says, taking the cotton fabric and placing it in one of several large bags sitting on the bamboo mat around her. Mama's in full initiation mode and with the weather officially warming up, it's just the beginning of her busy season as the head priestess in charge. All of the spiritual houses in Los Angeles County and beyond call on Mama's expertise, and I get to tag along as her assistant, even when I don't especially feel like it. I sit down in one of the chairs at the table and fan my face with my hand. It's a warm evening and with the way we threw down, the spirit room is still hot from the stove being on all day.

"Well, I guess I'd better get ready for the bembé," I say, looking up at the clock on the wall. We've been back here for hours, eating, talking, and laughing. The sweet spell I put on her and my mom at Daddy's church on Easter a couple of weeks ago has worked its magic and I couldn't have asked for a better outcome. I missed the last spiritual party celebrating the end of an initiation because of Misty's trifling ass. I'm not initiated yet and can't participate in all of the ins and outs of the rituals, but as Mama's apprentice I help in every other way. I was secretly hoping I'd start my cycle so I wouldn't have to help tonight, but no such luck. Any other time I'd be bleeding all over the place, but it's late this month. I wanted to take the time to catch up on my spirit work, focusing on my latest acquisition. Possessing my mom's gift of sight is a trip, and I want to learn more about controlling it. Keeping my newfound powers a secret has been no easy task, but so far, so good.

"I think your ashe is still too vulnerable to attend any spiritual festivities tonight, but there will be another bembé soon," Mama says, unknowingly granting my silent wish. She opens the spirit book sitting next to her and directs me to sit across from her on the mat. "Read that section and take a honey bath when you get . . . home," she says, faltering on her last word. Tears cloud Mama's jade eyes and fall to the page, permanently smudging the ancient black ink.

"Oh, Mama," I say, reaching across the mat to hug my

grandmother. I hate it when she cries. "I miss you, too." And I do. I also miss my grandfather Daddy, my cousin Jay, and my crazy uncle Bryan. It's the rest of the fools up in the house, my other uncles, I'm glad to be rid of.

"Why do I lose all of my girls?" Mama asks, holding me tightly. The faint scent of garlic and rosemary drifts up from her apron, tickling my nose. Both of her daughters moved out the first chance they got, and so did I. I can't speak for Jay's mama or mine, but Mama has to realize how hard it is being the only young woman in a houseful of men.

"It's not you. But living with all these dudes is a bit much," I say, holding on to Mama for one more second before letting go. Mama looks into my eyes, and I into hers, trying to use my mom's cooling gifts on her mind, but it's still no use. Mama's too powerful for my tricks. Luckily for me, her head's too hot with emotions to detect my attempted intrusions.

"I'd better get dressed before Netta gets here," Mama says, rising from the floor and making her way to the door. It's hard for Mama to understand why everyone can't be as strong as she is, just like I can't understand for the life of me why she chooses to stay with a husband who cheats on her and trifling sons who don't respect her house.

"Maybe you and I can get a place of our own," I say.

Mama smiles and kisses me on the cheek. "You are so sweet. And so young," she says, taking three of the bags and directing me to claim the other three from the mat.

I follow her out of the spirit room and into the main house. It's still too early in the evening for my uncles to come home and Daddy's probably having dinner at the church where he's the pastor. Bryan and Jay are watching television in the living room and look less than enthusiastic to see us walk through the kitchen door. We set the bags down on the dining room table, checking to make sure we've got everything.

"Have fun, Mama, and tell Netta I said hi," I say, kissing her on the cheek. Jay and Bryan look up and wave before returning their attention to the Bernie Mac rerun on the screen.

"Will do, baby, and see you tomorrow afternoon at work," Mama says, quickly hugging me before heading to her room to get dressed for the party. I'm sure she'll look brilliant in her all-white clothing, as always. "And don't forget your spirit work, Jayd," Mama yells from her room. Little does she know that's all I can think about. I'm looking forward to looking through the spirit book for more information on my mom's powers and clues as to how I can keep them. I have to be careful not to tip her or my mom off, or my new sight will be gone before I can master it, and I'm not ready for that yet. I want to be as dope as Mama is with her shit and as bad as my mom was when she had complete control of her mind-altering powers. And to get that flyy I've got a lot of work to do, starting right now.

~ 1 ~
Say What?

*"You can be as good as the best of them
but as bad as the worst/so don't test me.
You better move over."*

—NOTORIOUS B.I.G.

Since Mama's leaving for the evening, I'll take the opportunity to study the spirit book for a while. Making my way out of the kitchen and through the back yard, I notice Lexi, Mama's dog, following me to the backhouse. She takes her guardian job way too seriously, if you ask me. I open the screen door and lock it behind me lest anyone decide to surprise me back here, which I doubt. The boys rarely go any farther than the garage attached to the front of the small house. They don't know exactly what we do back here, nor do they want to.

"Finally, some alone time in the spirit room," I say to Lexi, who looks uninterested in my enthusiasm. I wish I could read her mind, but unfortunately my newfound sight doesn't work on dogs. I have a couple of hours before Jeremy meets me back at my mom's and I want to get as much work done as I can. Before I can get into my studying, my phone vibrates with another call from Rah. Now what?

"Hey, girl," Rah says groggily through my cell. When I left his house Friday night, he and Sandy were still going hard. I've got too much work to do today to be his shoulder, and need to make this call quick if I want to take full advantage of my alone time.

"What's up, Rah? I'm at Mama's," I say while turning from the page that Mama left open for me to study and search for my own shit. I'll take the bath as prescribed and do some of my assignment, but tonight it's all about my personal agenda.

"Can you come over on your way home? I have a little something for you I meant to give you Friday." He can't be serious. There's no way in hell I'm stepping back into his house as long as Sandy's Amazonian ass is there. "Sandy's gone to her grandparents' house for the weekend." Rah's no mind reader, but he hit that one on the head. I thought he told his baby-mama to move out, but I don't have time to get the full story.

"It'll have to be quick because I already have plans for the evening," I say, glancing at the wall clock and down at the work in front of me. It's going to take me at least a couple of hours to finish up here and I told Jeremy I'd be back at my mom's in Inglewood by nine, which means I'll have to leave here and get to Rah's by eight to make it back on time.

"Cool. See you later," Rah says. I hang up my cell and focus on the task at hand. I don't know why I keep bending to Rah's will, but I'm getting stronger in more ways than one. Besides, a gift is a gift and who am I to say no? A true friend forgives, and I have no problem with that. And as long as Rah doesn't mistake my kindness for weakness—again—it's all good.

It was nice working alone on my spirit work and it was just the peace I needed to get my mind right for the week ahead. I'm working extra hard to get Mama the stove she so deserves for Mother's Day and to make up for all the work I missed studying for my Advanced Placement exams last week. Luckily, summer's around the corner, and with both my main job at Netta's beauty shop and my side hustle doing hair at my mom's place, my cheddar should be well stacked in a few months.

It took me longer than normal to get back to the west side of town because of the Sunday cruisers out enjoying the beautiful evening. Maybe Jeremy and I can take a ride down the coast tonight if he's not too tired from surfing all day. Jeremy takes his chosen sport very seriously and with his competition coming up, he's been pushing harder than ever to be on top of his game.

I've been at Rah's house for all of ten minutes and already his cell phone is working my nerves. He's been in his room talking since I arrived, and I'm ready to go. If I leave now I could take a shower and relax before Jeremy arrives, not that he cares much how I look these days. We just like being together, morning breath, stank asses and all.

"Rah, I'm out," I shout from my stance in the living room and head toward the front door. The days of waiting for Rah's undivided attention are a thing of the past.

"Oh no, you don't," he says, jogging into the foyer with a small gold box in hand. He hangs up his cell and hands me my belated gift. Finally. My birthday was weeks ago, but just because it's late doesn't mean I won't accept it. I look up at my boy and smile, opening the box. Rah always gives thoughtful gifts.

"Oh, Rah, it's beautiful," I say, pulling out the gold ankh charm hanging from a matching chain. He's never bought me something so extravagant before. This bling must've set him back at least a bill or two. With my gold "Lady J" bangle from Jeremy, I'm starting myself a nice little collection of boyfriend jewelry, even if Rah is technically my ex. Mickey's the one with the jewelry box full of shiny things from all of her conquests, but my two pieces are nothing to laugh at.

"I know your birthday passed and I acted like a jackass,

but I still wanted to give you your gift," he says, taking the heavy necklace from my hands and walking behind me. "Let me help you put it on." I move my freshly pressed hair from my left shoulder to my right and hold it up slightly so he can see what he's doing. After securing the cold metal around my neck, Rah bends down and gently kisses me. He knows my neck is extra sensitive, especially in the groove between my ear and shoulder on either side.

"Rah, I've got a man, in case you forgot," I say, trying to resist his soft lips, but he ignores my reminder and keeps kissing, now almost sucking my skin. If he doesn't stop soon I'm going to have a hickey on my neck the size of Long Beach to explain to Mama and everyone else with eyes, including Jeremy.

"Do you really want me to stop?" Rah asks, moving his hips from side to side and me right along with him. Damn, he feels good; too good. His phone vibrates in his jean pocket and just in time, too. I almost got caught up in the rapture with this brotha and that is the wrong direction to go in.

"I've got to get this. Don't move," Rah says, stepping into the living room and leaving me shell-shocked in the foyer. I should really get going, but before I can make my escape I hear something in the back of the house. As Rah continues his conversation in the living room, Sandy walks into the kitchen through the studio door with Rahima on her hip. Why didn't she come in through the front door like she normally would? I don't care enough to ask, nor do I want to stick around for the show.

"I saw you two making out through the window," Sandy says—no hi or hello. Where are her manners? "Are you going to stand there and tell me that you didn't give up the panties yet?" Sandy asks, throwing her cell phone down on the counter. Rahima looks frightened but stays glued to her mother's side. Sandy has little regard for her young daughter.

"Well, hello to you, too," I say, waving at my girl, who waves back in her cute two-year-old way. It looks more like snatching than waving, but I'll take what I can get.

"Please, Jayd, y'all can cut the act. There's only one reason a nigga would deny all of this when it's right here in front of his face, and that's if he's getting ass from someone else." Sandy takes a pot out of the cabinet under the stove and walks over to the sink, filling it with water like she's about to cook, but we both know that's not what she's doing.

"Say what?" I ask, completely offended by her accusation, and so is Rah, who finally walks into the kitchen to deal with his irrational baby-mama. This is my final cue to roll.

"Sandy, you're talking like you're crazy. Did you take your meds today?" Rah asks, but there's nothing funny about Sandy's behavior. Rah reaches for his daughter, but as usual Sandy's holding her hostage to make her point. I can't be a party to this drama any more than I already am. And I'm pissed that someone witnessed my moment of infidelity. Even if I didn't initiate the neck kiss, I also didn't do anything to stop it. How am I going to explain this one to Jeremy, not to mention the new gold hanging from my neck?

"Don't play with me, fool. I know what I saw." Sandy's eyes are more evil than usual. I hope she's not planning to cook grits, because I do not want to witness an Al Green moment. Besides, she has no right reacting to Rah and me doing anything together, even if she's way off. Why is she the only one who doesn't see that?

Because she's right to some degree, my mom says telepathically, reasoning for the wrong side. Shouldn't she be kicking it with her own man instead of worrying about me and mine?

Mom, not now. Please. I can't tell, but I think my mom's

laughing at my plea to get her out of my mind. Like I have any control over that. Maybe I can work on that part of my vision, too. Now that I possess her sight, there has to be a way to control it.

"Sandy, you need to relax. You're not my wife and I don't have to answer to you—we already established that the last time you tried to pull this shit. We're not a family, Sandy," Rah says. His phone rings again and he goes back into the living room to answer it. Sandy looks at me like she wants to slit my throat with one of the knives by the stove. If I could fly over there I'd move them out of her reach, but no such luck.

"I've got to make a run real quick," Rah says, coming back into the foyer where I'm posted. "Jayd, you want to come with me?" I look from Sandy to Rah and then at the clock on the kitchen stove. Jeremy should be on his way soon and I don't want to keep him waiting. "Ten minutes, Jayd, I promise."

"All right," I agree. Anywhere is better than being here with Sandy, and I want to make it clear to Rah that he can't kiss me like that anymore. Jeremy and I are definitely one-on-one these days, and he needs to respect that. Rah reaches for his keys on the kitchen counter and Sandy promptly snatches them up, now holding them and their daughter hostage.

"Y'all ain't going nowhere," she says, throwing the keys out of the open kitchen window. If Rah's mom kept up with the house maintenance like a good homeowner, there would be a screen there, preventing at least that part of Sandy's erratic behavior.

"What the hell did you do that for?" Rah yells at a smiling Sandy. Rahima leaps from her mother's arms and runs to her father, who picks her up, holding her tight.

"I've got to go," I say, opening the door behind me and heading away from the ugly scene. I can holla at Rah later. He

puts Rahima down and heads out of the front door behind
me. I wave 'bye to Rahima, who's now back in her mother's
arms. Poor baby. She doesn't know which way to go, and I
feel her. But unlike Rahima, I can drive away from the scene
of the crime. Sandy runs out of the kitchen and through the
back door. Rah and I stare at each other as we hear his car
door slam and the engine start.

"'Bye, bitches!" Sandy yells, pulling away from the curb
and speeding down the street with Rahima in the backseat.
She must've found the keys to Rah's ride in the bushes. I told
Nellie black girls don't call another sistah a bitch without
meaning it in the worst way possible. I thought Rah learned
his lesson the last time she stole his grandfather's car, but I
guess not. If my dream about her driving fast and ultimately
getting into a near-fatal accident was any indication of what's
ahead, I need to warn Rah.

"We have to stop her," I say to him, but Rah just looks after
his red car speeding down the street, completely dazed. "Come
on," I say, running over to my mom's car parked in the driveway, but he doesn't move.

"Man, I'm done chasing that trick. Let her parole officer
catch her," Rah says, not realizing how serious the situation
is. He looks down at his ringing cell and silences it for the
moment. What the hell?

"Rah, Sandy's out of control and with your daughter in
the back. Don't you care about Rahima's well-being?" I open
the car door and get in, starting the engine. If we leave now
we may be able to catch Sandy at the light.

"That's what I'm saying," he says, sending a text to God-
only-knows who. "When she gets busted for being out past
her curfew, she'll be in violation of her parole and back in
jail, and I'll have Rahima once and for all. Besides, I've got
something to handle real quick. Can you drive, baby?" What
the hell did this fool just say to me? And is Rah seriously

putting his hustle over his daughter's safety in the hopes that Sandy will get busted? Really?

"Rah, I'm telling you that Sandy driving with Rahima is a bad idea. I had a dream about her getting into an accident where they both get seriously hurt." Rah gets into the passenger's seat and looks at me, stroking my cheek with his left hand.

"Jayd, Rahima's in the car with her mother every day, and nothing that bad has ever happened. Maybe your dream meant something else," he says, patronizing me. Rah's never going to take me seriously when it come to what's best for Rahima because I'm not her mother, and I see that clearly now. "Now can we go, please? That girl's already got me running late and I need to get my money."

"Find another way to get there. I'm going home," I say, pushing Rah out of my mom's ride and shutting the door behind him. I already know where this road leads and I refuse to go down it with him anymore. I've been way too nice about this entire situation, and however their mess ends, I want no part of it.

By the time Jeremy and I finally managed to fall asleep last night, it was too late for me to get a good night's rest. Rah always manages to get my head too hot for my own good. There has to be some way I can permanently protect myself from his advances, because Lord knows I've tried stopping Rah before, and each time I finally give in to his undeniable charm. Even if Rah is an arrogant and bold fool at times, I have to admit I love his taste in jewelry. I've been at school all day sporting my belated birthday gift and managing to hide it from Jeremy at the same time. I took the necklace off last night because I didn't want to explain to Jeremy where it came from, but that discussion is inevitable if I plan on keeping the gift. The solid gold feels good around my neck. Now

I know how Chance feels, sporting all of his rapper-like bling: It just feels good wearing a little weight.

"Good morning, class," Mrs. Sinclair, says, her frizzy red hair officially entering the room before she does. "Quiet down, quiet down," she says as we all file into the miniature rehearsal room that doubles as our main classroom. As we all settle into fifth period, Mrs. Sinclair looks overly excited to announce our final play of the school year. I didn't support the spring musical because, as usual, there were no leading roles for a sistah—let them tell it. But in order to maintain my A average, I have to participate in the last production of the year in some capacity. And to continue as an active thespian—or honors drama club member—I have to try out. Every club has its rules of engagement.

"What gives, Mrs. S?" Chance asks, making his favorite teacher's cheeks the same color as her hair.

"The spring play will be *Wait until Dark* by Frederick Knott. I am so thrilled! I love this script," she says, passing out xeroxed copies to half of the class and playbooks to the other half. She only has enough original scripts for the cast members. I snatch up a book and Chance grabs a copy. Everyone's already visualizing who he or she'll be, including me. Hopefully I'll have a good chance at the lead.

"Shit," I say under my breath, but it doesn't escape Chance's ears.

"What's wrong?" he asks, looking through his packet. "I'm definitely trying out as one of the bad guys in the opening scene," he says, already absorbed in the dialogue.

"The lead is a blind woman," I say, looking through the cast description. "And the only other female role is a little girl. What the hell am I supposed to do with this?" Being blind is a taboo for the women in my lineage—even while pretending, I assume.

"Of course you will need to prepare a dialogue and a

monologue for auditions, which will begin next week. Get busy, young people." Mrs. Sinclair leaves us to our reading and heads back to the theater.

"So, which scene are we going to perform, my blind lady?" Chance says, not realizing that his playful comment gives me the chills. I never want to be blind again—for real or fiction. My sleepwalking incident a few months ago, where I lost my sight temporarily, was enough for me.

"Chance, that's not funny. And I'm not trying out for the lead. I'm going for the little girl," I say, skimming through the ancient playbook. I've always liked the play, and Mama loved the movie with one of her favorite actresses, Audrey Hepburn, in the lead. Truthfully, I would love to play the lead role, but I can't take the risk.

"The hell you are," Chance says, snatching the playbook out of my hand and writing my name next to the lead role. "There. Now you have to try out. Let's get to work picking a scene."

"I appreciate the faith, Chance, but you know I'm not going to get it anyway," I say, reaching for my script. "And I actually like the little girl. Gloria's got balls." Both women in the play have gumption, and I like the plot. "As long as I can be in the last production of the year, I'm good." Chance's blue eyes look like they're trying to probe my mind, but he doesn't have it like the women in my family do.

"Jayd, I don't get you. One minute you're up in arms about there not being any parts for you and how unfair the school is. The next you're turning down the perfect part for you. What the hell?" Alia, Cameron, Matt, and Seth busy themselves with discussing the set designs and other behind-the-scenes details for the production. We have six weeks left in school and the final performance is usually the week before the last, which means our rehearsal schedule will be tight for the next four weeks. The remainder of the class files outside and into the dressing rooms to begin rehearsals. Everyone has to try out: no exceptions. And even if there aren't enough parts, Mrs. Sinclair makes it a point to have groups perform during class time for grades. That way everyone participates and she has a good pool of understudies if need be.

"Chance, it's complicated," I say, looking down at my vibrating phone to see a text from Rah. Ever since his little fiasco with Sandy last night, I've been giving him the cold shoulder. This fool is tripping if he thinks I'm going out like a sucker. I have a man and he's a good one. It's high time I started acting like it, and that includes no more drama with Rah.

"Yeah, I see," Chance says, looking at my phone and then back up at me. "When are you going to get a new phone?"

"Why would I do that when I just got this one for Christmas?" I ask, silencing my cell.

"Because you got it from him," Chance says, pointing at the open door where Rah walks in with Nigel behind him. What the hell is he doing here? Doesn't he know he's on the student roster at Westingle High, not South Bay?

"Oh shit," I say under my breath. The last thing I want is an argument. I have too much work to do and I need to keep my head clear for work this afternoon. Mama and Netta have a long list of things for me to do at Netta's shop because they're busy with religious duties these days, and I'm grateful for the extra cash. I still haven't got completely back on point financially because of all the time I took off studying for the Advanced Placement exams, but I'm getting back on my game.

"What's he doing here?" I ask aloud like I don't already know the answer to the question. As usual, Rah wants to apologize for his rude-ass behavior.

"Jayd," Nigel says, waving for me to come over. And why isn't he in class, too? It must be nice being an athlete and enjoying all the perks thereof.

"I'm busy, in case you didn't notice the classroom you just walked into." I do my best to ignore them both and return my attention to Chance, who is busy texting. Fine. In the meantime I'll pick out my own scene to perform by myself.

"Jayd, it'll only take a minute," Rah says, pleading with those brown, puppy dog eyes that always get him his way—but not this time. I'm too pissed at the disrespect he showed me yesterday and at the fact that he didn't heed my warning. Between Sandy and me, I am obviously the more trustworthy, but Rah still brushed me off because I'm not Rahima's mom and never will be, no matter how much I care about her.

"You really to need to handle him, Jayd, before Mrs. Sinclair comes back in here and has a fit," Chance says, putting his BlackBerry back in its holder on his pants buckle. "Come on, you know I've got your back." Chance rises from his seat and reaches his hand out for me to take. His Rolex watch dangles loosely on his thin wrist, reminding me of his mother's matching watch. I wonder if she's told him the truth about his adoption yet? I love my boy and I hope he finds out about his black blood sooner than later. Thanks to my dreams, I know more about my friend than I want to. I don't know how much longer I can keep a secret this big.

"I guess you're right," I say, reluctantly rising from my spot and heading toward the front door. Students are outside, loudly rehearsing their scenes and talking in general. I love drama class. It's the most expressive elective offered at this school, and I fit right in here, most of the time.

"Thank you," Rah says, hugging me tightly, knowing I've already forgiven him when he is so wrong.

"For what?" I ask, pushing him away. "I came out here to

warn you before our teacher comes back in the room. Every-one ain't as cool as Mr. Adewale," I say, reminding him and Nigel that the only black male teacher up here, who just hap-pened to referee an off-campus game for them months ago, is about as good as it gets. All the other teachers couldn't give a shit about a hall pass when it comes to black male stu-dents roaming around campus.

"I know you're pissed about what happened last night and I'm sorry. What do you want me to do?" Rah asks, throw-ing his hands in the air like this bull isn't his own making. "Sandy should've never seen us kissing, Jayd. I knew that would set her off, but she wasn't supposed to be there, I promise." I look from Rah to Chance, who looks shocked by Rah's confession. Jeremy is Chance's best friend, and I know he's wondering if Jeremy knows about Rah kissing me—which he doesn't, and I need to keep it that way.

"First of all, you snuck in a kiss on the neck; I did not kiss you back," I say, vindicating myself from his implication of joint responsibility. I want to make it very clear I had nothing to do with his affection. "And second of all, I'm more pissed at the fact you didn't listen to me when I gave you a warning about your crazy-ass baby-mama." I look around, noticing we're causing a scene of our own.

"Okay, I know you were worried about Rahima and I re-spect that, Jayd, really I do. But I have to be able to trust her own mother with her well-being—otherwise I'd go crazy worrying about baby girl all the time." Rah looks around like he's expecting the school security to come and grab him at any moment, as well he should. Hall pass or not, if we get too loud they'll gladly snatch us all up.

"And that's fine with me because I couldn't care less. I'm out of it," I say, turning around to head back inside. We have a good twenty minutes left in fifth period and I want to use it productively, not out here arguing with Rah.

"Jayd, you don't mean that. You know you're Rahima's godmother as far as I'm concerned, and she loves you, too."

"Good try, but I'm not falling for your bull anymore, Rah. I'm out." Before I can get away, Rah takes my hand, forcing me to turn around. Chance looks up and sees what I see: Jeremy turning red at the sight of Rah and me holding hands. Oh shit.

"What's up, man?" Jeremy asks, stepping up to Rah and claiming my hand in his own. I've never seen Jeremy look so pissed before. How did he know what was going on all the way down here? Jeremy's chemistry class is on the other side of campus in the science hall. Because the theater department is at the bottom of the massive campus, no one ever comes down here without intending to. Maybe that's who Chance was texting a moment ago.

"We were just talking," Rah says, reluctantly letting me go. He knows he has no right to claim me, especially not with my new man standing eye to eye with him, obviously ready to do whatever's necessary to make his point clear.

"Please don't let me stop you. What are we talking about?" Jeremy asks, holding my right hand in his while he wraps his left arm around my shoulder, completely engulfing me in his protective embrace. Nigel looks at us in disbelief. I bet he never thought he'd see the day Rah had to let me go to a white boy. Oh well. I've got ninety-nine problems and a fool ain't one—anymore.

"Never mind," Rah says, backing down for the moment. He looks at the gold necklace and charm he planted on me last night and I instinctively begin to play with the heavy ankh. "I just wanted to reiterate how sorry I was that I missed your birthday and I hope you like your gift. Peace." Rah nods his head in Chance's direction and gives Jeremy a hard look, which Jeremy returns. They were never very fond of each other, but I was hoping they would at least be able to grow to tolerate one another. I think that ship has permanently sailed.

"I'll holla at y'all later," Nigel says, following Rah back toward the parking lot. Nigel's supposed to be at basketball practice right now. But because football is his first love, he slacks off in B-ball a lot, unlike KJ and his crew, who live for this season. They made it to the finals and will be ready to take it to the state championships before it's all said and done. Their only real challenge is Westingle, and that game is coming up soon. Nigel knows all of those cats, too, and I'm sure his loyalty is split, just like it is between his newfound friends here and his old friends there, like Rah.

"What the hell was that all about?" Jeremy asks, relaxing his stance a little bit now that Rah's disappeared off campus.

"Do you want the short version or the long one?" I ask, looking at Chance's watch for the time. Neither Jeremy nor I wear watches, and I left my phone in the room with the rest of my belongings.

"Whichever one includes Rah giving you this," Jeremy says, flicking the gold charm with his middle finger. "Why didn't you tell me he gave this to you?" I look into Jeremy's magnetic blue eyes and wish I had the opportunity to chill his mind out and tell him what all went down last night, but there's no time. The bell's about to ring and we all have to get back inside.

"I was going to, but I didn't know what to say." Chance makes a sound indicating I'm not being completely honest and he's right. But damn, did he have to sell me out like that?

"You don't know what to say? Since when? I'll let it slide for now, Lady J, but we need to talk about this." Jeremy kisses me on the nose before jogging back up the hill.

"What the hell, Chance?" I ask, socking my homeboy in his arm. "I didn't tell Nellie about your little date at the beach last weekend. What the hell are you trying to do, break us up?"

"No. The exact opposite. If there's nothing to hide then spill it. Otherwise it's just lying, and I know Jeremy. If there's one thing he can't tolerate, it's being lied to for whatever reason." I know he's right and I didn't really do anything, but I still feel guilty. "Tania lied to him about being pregnant, and then when he finally did find out, the bitch was already engaged and making baby plans without him. He's never gotten over it and won't. I know this isn't as serious, but it's still a lie, Jayd, and you need to clear it up—fast." We walk back into the room and take our seats with the rest of the class. Mrs. Sinclair has reentered the room, talking with the groups individually about their casting and scene choices, which Chance and I are still mulling over.

This isn't like me, and I'm the last person I want to remind Jeremy of his ex-baby-mama, Tania. The only thing that makes his situation more dignified than Rah's is money. Otherwise, I'm sure they'd have similar issues. Maybe I can explain it to him tonight after work. But right now, I have to get back on my grind and let the energy pass because, as of now, Jayd Jackson is officially back on her shit. And that starts with choosing the best audition monologue and scene.

Well, I'm certainly glad to hear that, my mom says, interrupting my reading. *And don't worry about your audition, Jayd. I don't think you'll go blind again by playing a blind woman. It doesn't work like that, and besides, what are your jade bracelets for? Use them and have faith.* 'Bye, my mom says, checking out of my head.

Maybe everything will be okay and I'm tripping for nothing. Still, I'm not sure if this part's for me, but I'll try it out for size. If I never challenge myself—even when it's not necessarily my thing—I'll never grow, and that's what I'm here for. I love my hoods, but I don't want to stay in Compton or Inglewood forever. College is my preferred way out, and doing as many notable activities in high school as possible is my way into the University of West LA. So if I have to try out for tainted lead roles or drink expensive tea at debutante meetings all day long to get in, I'm on it.

~ 2 ~
Cup of Tea

"If I was a rich girl."
—GWEN STEFANI

After working at Netta's shop all afternoon and well into the evening, I was too tired to move when I got back to Inglewood. Of course Mama tried to convince me to spend the night in Compton because it was so late when we left the shop, but all I wanted to do was soak in a long, hot bath and call it a night. My mom's quiet apartment is always the path of least resistance, even with all of the spirit work and homework I have on my plate, because my mom's always at her boyfriend Karl's place.

I spent an hour last night getting myself organized for the week ahead and finally took a bath and called it a night. I'm praying that I make it through to the end of the school year as drama-free as possible. I know I just have to keep pushing and it'll be all right. Unlike these rich folks up here at South Bay High, I have to work hard for mine and I don't mind one bit. I'm used to it. If one of these privileged rich girls had to live a day in my shoes, she'd probably break down and cry.

I don't know why Mr. Adelizi wants to see me this morning. I've been on my game academically all year long—as always—and I'm sure he's well aware of my Advanced Placement exams being complete. It's too early to choose classes for my senior year, so what the hell does he want?

Maybe the scores for the AP exams are in early. I'm anxious to
see what I got on all three of my exams, but they're not due
for another week or two.

I walk through the nearly empty main hall toward the
main office, thankful to have escaped government class for
the remainder of third period. My first two classes were
pretty uneventful, and Jeremy and I spent the nutrition
break together avoiding the looming conversation about
Rah's impromptu school visit yesterday and belated birthday
gift still hanging around my neck. Usually Jeremy's pretty
laid-back about everything, but seeing me with another dude
always gets his feathers ruffled. I could tell he needed to cool
off before bringing the subject up again and I'm happy to
wait as long as possible to have that conversation.

I step into the main office and head straight for the counselors' offices. There are five counselors on campus: one for
each grade level and an extra one for "special circumstances." Luckily I haven't been in that office at all this semester and I'm trying hard to keep it that way. But broads
like Misty, my former best friend turned worst enemy, and
Laura, the rich white bitch from hell, make it difficult to
maintain my cool. Hopefully I won't run into Misty or her
mama this morning. She works in the attendance office. I've
never had a problem with Miss Caldwell, but now that she's
under the influence of my crazy next-door neighbor and
Mama's enemy, Esmeralda, I don't want to take any chances.

"Miss Jackson, it's good to see you. Have a seat," Mr.
Adelizi, the junior class counselor, says, gesturing for me to
sit down in the only available seat in the cramped space. I
guess the end-of-the-year paperwork has overwhelmed him a
bit because the other student seat is stacked with folders and
so is every other available space in his office, including his
desk. Even his chair has a bag hanging from the arm with

overflowing pages hitting his left elbow. Don't they have housekeeping every evening in the main office?

"What's up, Mr. Adelizi?" I ask, trying to avoid as much small talk as possible. Coming to the counselor's office is always uncomfortable to me. It usually symbolizes some sort of change, and if it's not voluntary or positive, I'm really not in the mood to deal with it.

"Well, Jayd, I've been reviewing your transcripts and you should think about adding more diverse activities to your academic resume if you're still planning on applying to colleges in the fall," he says, pointing at the computer screen in front of him. If I add any more activities to my already full schedule I might go crazy.

"Mr. Adelizi, if you see what I see, I already have a full plate," I say, squinting at the screen. Lately my vision hasn't been very clear. Maybe I just need more rest. I have been up reading late and my mom's apartment doesn't have the best lighting for studying, since most of her light consists of low lamps and candles. It's a great atmosphere for relaxing but horrible for getting any work done.

That's because it's a grown woman's apartment, not a high school student's, my mom says, all up in my business this morning. *And stop complaining. If you need more light, buy yourself a desk lamp or brighter bulbs. There's a Target up the street.*

I wasn't complaining, Mom, and please get out of my head. I'm in a meeting with my counselor, I say, staring at Mr. Adelizi, who's concentrating on my transcripts. Thank God, because I still haven't mastered hiding the distant look on my face when my mom's in my head; yet another thing I need to work on.

"Well, how about cheer?" he asks, handing me one of the fluorescent pink fliers posted all over the campus and ending the psychic conversation in my head. I look at the bright pink and green paper, grateful I don't have to hand these out. I'm getting a headache just reading the damn thing.

"Come again?" He must not know me at all, no matter how much he pretends to be in tune with his students. Obviously he's been gravely misinformed about Jayd Jackson.

"Weren't you on the spirit squad last year?" Mr. Adelizi asks, reminding me of my brief attempt at joining the lesser of the school spirit teams. That was at the beginning of my sophomore year, before I had my breast reduction surgery, which changed more than my appearance: It also gave me more confidence and a new outlook on my social life.

"I was, but only for a few weeks. It wasn't my thing." I can still smell the sweat of a thousand other students who wore the school mascot costume before me, which the members rotated wearing every week. It's one thing to do it every now and then for fun, but to have to wear the large, two-piece sea-hawk costume for three hours straight is pure torture.

"But you were in dance class for the last two semesters and that seemed to work well for you, or does Ms. Carter simply hand out A's to all of the students?" Mr. Adelizi can be a real smart-ass when he wants to.

"No, I earned that grade." And I did. Ms. Carter's a tough teacher and I miss the creative and physical workouts her classes gave me. I've noticed my pants getting a little tighter around the waist since her class was discontinued last semester, and Jeremy constantly feeding me isn't helping the situation much, either. Now she's the full-time cheer squad coordinator. But I'm still not going to be a pom-pom girl.

"Okay then. Sign-ups start today after school," Mr. Adelizi continues, still not feeling me.

"Mr. Adelizi, I'm already in the drama club, speech and debate, and the African Student Union, not to mention I work two jobs. I don't have time for anything else, but thanks for your concern," I say, rising from my seat. But apparently he's not through with me yet.

"Miss Jackson, I remember the first time we spoke about your attending college and I was less than supportive, and for that, I'm sorry," Mr. Adelizi says, signaling me to reclaim my seat. I'm in no rush to get back to government class, so I'll gladly stay until the bell rings. After that, I'm out whether he's in midsentence or not.

"It's cool," I say. I was over that shit the day it happened. When I first came to South Bay High, with its rich, white population, I knew where I was and didn't expect anything more or less from the administration up here. And unfortunately, Mr. Adelizi was partially correct to jump to the conclusion that I might not want to attend college. Out of my hood crew, I'm the only one who wants to attend college. Nigel's automatically going, but sports are his motivation, not academics or upward social mobility, because his parents are already doing well financially. Rah will probably go, but if he doesn't get in it won't be a big deal to him. And as for my girls, they never even considered going to school any longer than they have to.

"No, it's not. I made an assumption about you based on your economic background and that wasn't fair." Mr. Adelizi looks truly repentant for his racist ways, but why now? There has to be a catch.

"To be honest, I'm used to it. It shocks me more when people don't size me up when they find out I'm from Compton." We stare at each other for a moment, unsure of who should speak next. I'm sure he wasn't expecting such a blunt response, but again, he doesn't know me at all.

"Excuse me, Mr. Adelizi. There's a call for you on line two," one of the school secretaries says, stepping into the open door and breaking the awkward silence.

"Can you please tell them I'll be just a moment?" Mr.

Adelizi looks at my transcripts on the computer screen in front of him and back at me. "Jayd, I'm impressed with your tenacity. You've kept up with your Advanced Placement courses and you continue to stay active in drama, but that's not going to be enough to make you stand out as a well-rounded candidate for the top colleges, which I hope you're still considering applying to come fall." Mr. Adelizi looks down at the blinking phone on his crowded desk and back up at me, hoping his words have sunk in.

"Trust me, it's all I think about." The sooner I get out of high school, the better. And from what I heard KJ's older friends say about college life when KJ and I were together, and from what Mr. Adewale's shared about his experiences, University of West Los Angeles is the place to be, and that's where I plan on going. I've never been to the campus, but I'm sure it's all that and then some.

"That's good to hear. There are many colleges that are looking to broaden the diversity of their student population. That said, they are looking for top candidates from the local distinguished high schools first. Now, I have placed your name on that list for South Bay and hope you're open to the program."

"It sounds like a good opportunity, Mr. Adelizi. Thank you," I say, surprised that I was called into his office for good news rather than the usual bull.

"But there's a catch," Mr. Adelizi says, cocking his pale chin forward with a stern look of caution. I knew there was more to it. He almost got me off my game, but not completely. "Your records have a few minor negatives that need to be balanced out. I suggest you either join a sport or cheer. Either will show you can be a team player and that's an important character trait. That little temper of yours can be played down if your activities are more varied."

"I'll think about joining another club or something, but

truthfully, cheerleading isn't my cup of tea." The bell signaling the end of third period rings and that's my cue to roll out. I don't want to be late for Mr. Adewale's class, even though we have a quiz in speech and debate this afternoon. It's always a pleasure to see him.

"But how will you know until you try?" Was this dude listening to the conversation I had with myself yesterday about trying out for Susy, the lead role in the spring play? Could Mr. Adelizi actually be on to something with cheer? "Think outside the box, Jayd. That's what colleges look for in serious candidates." Mr. Adelizi takes the call and leaves me to mull over my options.

Is my future here already? College always felt so far away from high school, but my senior year is around the corner. I'll be out on my own soon and I want to have the best options available to me. Wait until my crew finds out that I, Jayd Jackson, Miss "I hate all things ASB, athletes and cheerleaders" is thinking of joining the enemy. I'll really be coined a traitor then.

The quiz in fourth period took up the majority of class time, leaving my crew and me no time to chat. It's a hot, sunny day and everyone's outside eating. So far, Nellie has dominated the lunch conversation, sharing all the vivid details of her first Lamaze class with Mickey and Nigel. They're required to have a backup labor partner for Mickey just in case the father's not there, and Nellie jumped at the chance to take control of another aspect of Mickey's pregnancy. If I can get a word in edgewise, I can lay out the news about pom-poms in my future for everyone to laugh at. Maybe they'll even talk me out of it. It's a silly idea, me a cheerleader in the short skirts and tight sweaters, screaming *Go, team, go!* in front of a crowd. No, not me. It may be fun sometimes, but I can't imagine becoming one of them.

Nellie takes a break from her chattering about the latest breathing techniques to ease labor pains to take a sip of her Diet Coke, finally allowing me the chance to share my news.

"I'm thinking about trying out for cheer," I say in between Doritos. Chance, Jeremy, and Nigel all look as shell-shocked as I feel for even considering it.

"Shut up," Nellie says, overexcited. "Me too! Finally, one of you is getting involved in the right kind of extracurricular activities. The drama club is so strange," Nellie says, primping in her MAC compact mirror. I guess she needs to be perfect for her Associated Student Body meeting in a few minutes. It's the last six weeks of school and ASB is in overdrive trying to raise money for prom and the rest of the end-of-the-year activities, including the cheer tryouts next week.

"I didn't know ASB members had to try out for their own activities," I say, confused about the process. I've never wanted to be a cheerleader, but since dance class is over it might be fun to show off my dance skills in another way. I do miss making up routines. Weight lifting is cool but boring. If I make cheer, that will be my PE for next year and that sounds good to me.

"Of course we do. And besides, I know I'll make it whether I'm an Associated Student Body member or not," Nellie says like she's an officer of the group. Nellie won Homecoming princess for the junior class—not an actual election—making her an honorary member for the rest of the year. If Nellie doesn't find another way into ASB's tight-knit social and political circle, she'll be out. Speaking of which, we're voting for ASU officers soon and I need to make sure my speech as a candidate for president is on point. Even my haters will find it difficult to ignore the truth. I just hope they vote for it, too.

"Hey, y'all want to come by after school and kick it for a while? We haven't had a good session in a while," Nigel asks, looking at all of us. He's in an unusually good mood and I didn't even have to cool him off. What gives?

"Okay, what did I miss?" I ask, completely shocked by the mellow mood everyone's in. The last time I checked, Nigel was still in shock over Mickey finally admitting the baby she's carrying is Tre's, and Nellie and Mickey couldn't stand my ass because their boyfriends' mamas happen to like me, but I was able to calm them down. I didn't have anything to do with Nigel's newfound cool. Maybe because Tre, a gangster from our hood, saved Nigel from getting shot by Mickey's ex-man, he can live with his girl having Tre's baby.

"Nothing," Mickey says, kissing her man's cheek like they're back in love. Whatever the case, I'm just glad they're back on point. I know my goddaughter is happy in Mickey's belly, too. She looks like she's going to make her appearance sooner than later. Her parents need to get with the program, and it seems like they finally have.

"Yeah, it's all good, Jayd. Chance, you down?" Nigel asks, getting the tally from everyone for the spontaneous after-school session. I wonder if Jeremy's invited even if Rah shows up, which is quite probable.

"Yeah, man. Why not?" Chance says, kissing Nellie before she walks off toward the main hall. I know he's thinking the same thing most of us are: Where's the real Nellie, and who is this imposter who took over her head? Nellie had the most beautiful jet-black hair, and now the blonde has completely taken over.

"I can't. Got surf practice. That reminds me, our competition is next Saturday. Hope you guys can make it," Jeremy says, smiling down at me. I still can't believe there's such a thing as a surf competition, but I'm there to support my man.

"Cool, man. I got you," Chance says with a strange pitch in his voice, like he's trying to change the way he speaks. Something's up with my friend and I can feel he wants to talk about it. I'll have to check on Chance when we get a minute alone, which is rare. But I can still call him and chat if I have to. There goes the bell. Lunch always seems to go by fast, but it's especially quick this afternoon because of the short Tuesdays for the weekly faculty meetings.

"All right, y'all. My house after school it is. Jayd, after work, girl. Promise you'll come kick it with your peeps," Nigel says, making me feel loved. How can I say no to an invitation like that, even if a sistah's going to be wiped out after getting off work at Netta's this evening? But a girl needs to chill, too.

"Bet. I'll see y'all later," I say, shaking the grass off my jeans before grabbing my backpack and heading down the hill to drama class. I'd much rather eat pizza and watch movies with my friends than sign up for cheer this afternoon. Luckily, it's Mama's solo hair day at the shop when Netta does only Mama's hair, and there won't be any other clients to take care of, making my job easier this afternoon. A kick-it session with the crew is just what I need to ease up on planning my future and enjoy my present.

I missed talking to Jeremy this afternoon because I was so busy at Netta's. As soon as I arrived, Mama and Netta had a grip of laundry for me to do, as well as other tedious tasks resulting from the aftermath of their initiations this past weekend. I've never seen so many white clothes and other fabrics. I was so glad to get out of there for the night. It's almost eight and Nigel has assured me there's still plenty of Domino's pizza and breadsticks left over. I'm grateful because I'm starving.

I pull into Nigel's gated community off Crenshaw Boulevard, instantly aware I'm turning into the money side of South Central, the local hood. It's funny how just on the other side of this fancy brick and iron gate there are homeless people, and three families living in one house they're so strapped for cash. Driving into Lafayette Square is like going back in time to where families were supposedly picture-perfect, like the two- and three-story refurbished homes they live in. I park in front of Nigel's picturesque home, ready to get my grub on and watch *Gladiator* in high definition for the fiftieth time.

Walking up the driveway I can see Mickey, Nigel, and Mrs. Esop, Nigel's mom, in the foyer through the screen door, and it doesn't look pretty. I hope whatever's going on doesn't come between dinner and me.

I knock twice before entering, knowing it's already unlocked for me. I just want to warn everyone I'm coming through the door in case they want to censor their conversation and let a sistah pass by in peace.

"Yes, I am well aware of the true paternity of the child in question," Mrs. Esop says, looking at Mickey like she took a shit on the shiny hardwood floors. So much for me getting straight to the food. I wave to everyone, noticing Nellie and Chance in the living room witnessing the exchange I just walked in the middle of.

"Okay then, so stop tripping, Mom. Please." Nigel looks from Mickey's stomach to his mother's eyes and she softens her glare. "Tre took a bullet for me. If it weren't for him, I might not be here right now. The least I can do is raise his seed like it's my own, and that's exactly what I'm going to do." Nigel grabs Mickey around the waist, unable to fully fasten his fingers around her, but he's made his point. Nigel's not letting go now or ever, and that's good news to us all, except for Mrs. Esop.

"Nigel, I am grateful for the boy saving your life, but we don't owe her or that thug's child a damn thing." Mrs. Esop is no joke. "Now, this discussion is over. There will be no babies or baby-mamas in this house or their mother's." Mickey looks at Nigel, horrified by his mother's stance. Mickey was counting on Nigel being her ticket out of the hood and her parents' full house. I hate to lay it on my girl, but her plan was never a sure thing. I hope she's got a back-up arrangement because if not, she and her baby will be sleeping in her parents' living room.

"Mom, I'm not letting this go," Nigel says to his mother, who's halfway up the first flight of stairs. Her and her husband's suite is on the third floor of the massive home. There's plenty of room, none of which Mrs. Esop's willing to share with Mickey, no matter what her son says.

Looking back at us and smiling at her son's vehemence, Mrs. Esop looks at me as if her son didn't say a word.

"Jayd, I'll see you at the tea on Sunday. And please dress appropriately. It's customary for our debutantes to dress as the young ladies they are becoming," she says, looking from me to Mickey and then walking up the remaining stairs. Mrs. Esop's so serious about her shit. I'm actually starting to admire her no-nonsense swagger. If nothing else, Mrs. Esop's consistent about what she's about and what she's not. I could learn a lot from that kind of thinking. But Mickey's not feeling Nigel's mama at all, or the fact that Mrs. Esop obviously favors me over her.

"You're such an ass kissing little heffa, you know that?" Mickey says to me as if I went after Mrs. Esop on my own accord, forgetting whose idea it was for me to suck up to Nigel's mom in the first place.

"Mickey, I'm not having this argument with you again," I say, walking into the living room and putting my purse on the couch. Mickey and Nigel follow me into the large space, standing near the couch across from the television screen. "The whole reason I agreed to be in the cotillion was to get Mrs. Esop to come to your baby shower, which she did. Don't shoot the messenger, Mickey. I did my job." I walk toward the kitchen through the formal dining area to wash my hands before eating. Mickey follows me, ready to unleash all her anger for Mrs. Esop on me because I'm an easy target. I don't care what she says, as long as I get my food.

"Jayd, you're supposed to help me, not get in bed with my enemy," Mickey says. If I had the time I'd tell her how silly her point of view is on so many different levels, but I can't deal with her reasoning tonight.

"I'm not getting in bed with anyone, Mickey. But I am getting tired of always being the bad one. Can I eat and watch the movie now, or do you want to keep blaming me for your beef with Nigel's mom?" Mickey looks at me walking out of the kitchen without waiting for her answer. She knows she's out of line. Scratching her growing belly, Mickey walks back into the living room and claims her space next to her man on the couch. I sit in one of the two oversized chairs across from the loveseat Chance and Nellie are sharing, ready to relax, when I notice Rah's missing. I'm not even going to ask where he is if no one's offering to tell me. Like Mickey, Rah needs to grow up and deal with the real. Until they do, I have to keep my friends at arm's length because I'm ready to spread my wings and fly, right after I eat a couple of slices and chill out for the rest of the evening.

~ 3 ~
Stretch Marks

"I'll always come back to you."
—ISLEY BROTHERS

*C*arrying water on my head like one of my African fore-mothers, I balance the clay jug expertly, holding the right side with my hand and placing my left arm out by my side, helping me still my heavy load. Reaching my destina-tion—a small, one-room house—I open the curtained entry-way and place the jug down on the floor, rushing over to the woman lying on the bed straight ahead. There's blood everywhere and she's breathing hard and gripping the once white sheets with all her might.

"I can't take it anymore. The baby's never going to come," the laboring woman says in tears. She looks scared and overwhelmed. I get closer to her, hoping that I can pro-vide her with some comfort, recognizing the woman as Chance's birth mother. The dream I had months ago of the day he was adopted was the beginning of my knowing his family secret.

"It's time. Wet these towels to clean the baby when it comes," the elder midwife says from the corner of the room. She sounds like Mama and has the same feel as Mama does, but she doesn't look like my grandmother at all. This sistah is tall and thick with the same ebony complexion my mother has.

"Yes, ma'am," I say, taking the white towels from her and soaking them in the tepid water. I ring the water out, seeing my reflection in the clear liquid, and don't recognize myself, either. I look like I could be the midwife's daughter.

"I'm going to need for you to push as hard as you can now," the midwife says, holding Chance's mother's legs back while the laboring woman lifts her shoulders off the bed and gives it her all. But it's not enough. The young mother's exhausted and can't take any more pushing, but the baby has to be born.

"I'll help you push," Mrs. Carmichael, Chance's adoptive mother, says, appearing by the laboring mother's side and placing both hands on the bulging stomach, helping to push the baby out on the next contraction. "There he is," Mrs. Carmichael says, looking at Chance's infant self in the midwife's hands. "My son."

"Your son? He's my baby," Chance's birth mother says, looking at Mrs. Carmichael like an imposter instead of the woman who ends up raising Chance as her own child. She and Chance are closer than any mother and teenager I know. Mrs. Carmichael lets go of the angry woman's stomach, looking dead at me, her eyes red with pain.

"Jayd, help me, please! I'm losing my son," Mrs. Carmichael pleads, looking me in the eye, but I feel like she's actually talking to me outside of my dream. The urgency in her eyes reaches my core, making me feel partially responsible for Chance's identity crisis. I have to help them both if I can. The midwife hands the baby to his mother to nurse, leaving Mrs. Carmichael completely out of the first bonding ritual between a mother and child.

"No! He's my baby. He's mine," Mrs. Carmichael says, fading into the background from where she first appeared. Again, Mrs. Carmichael looks dead at me, now clearly in *my head. "Jayd, don't let them take away my son. Please, I need you."*

"What the hell?" I say, shaking out of my sleep and almost hitting my head on the coffee table I neglected to push away from the couch that doubles as my bed. I was so exhausted after hanging with Jeremy last night and my friends the night before that I couldn't be bothered with taking the usual environmental precautions. I just wanted to sleep. Had I known I was going to experience a crazy dream like that, I might not have been so anxious to rest.

I've been meaning to talk to Chance all week, but he's been very evasive lately. Today I'll make it a point to catch up with my friend, come hell or high water. But first I have to get the day started, and that means getting to school. Jeremy and I have gotten into such a good groove it's hard to know when to quit. If I keep having late nights like we did last night, it's going to make me unproductive and we can't have that.

Our late-night sessions are also affecting Jeremy. I hope he was able to get up this morning. He's been practicing for his surf competition every afternoon, and for an hour every morning before school. I'd be surprised if he makes it to school today. I, on the other hand, have to get going regardless of my exhaustion. I have a long school day ahead of me as well as having to work all evening. Some people look forward to Friday as their chill day. For me it's the beginning of my weekend grind, and I'm ready.

Today is the last day for cheer tryouts and I still don't know what to do. I watched some of the cheerleaders practicing yesterday during sixth period and they actually looked like they were having fun. There are two black girls on the varsity squad and they hold it down. Because they are a part of ASB and seniors, I've never really talked to them, although we say hi on the rare occasion that we do run into each other. They don't hang out in South Central, where the other two dozen or so black students hang, and because they all have white boyfriends and friends, I just assumed they were the girls that Nellie aspired to be like: as close to white as black girls can get.

I hate to admit it, but my thinking may have been wrong in more ways than one. Is it possible that I might have fun as a cheerleader? I don't know, but it may be worth a shot. And if I don't make it, at least I tried, and that might be enough to let Mr. Adelizi know I'm serious about being in the college program. I'll sign up for tryouts at break and see how it goes from there.

After my crazy dream about Chance last night, I really need to find him and make sure everything's all right with my friend. He's been going through it lately and I don't know exactly how to help him, but I want to try cooling Chance's mind a little bit now that I'm getting the hang of my mother's powers. I've already called him twice and sent him a text, all to no avail. I usually run into Chance before first period, but he's nowhere to be found. Maybe his girlfriend will know where her man's hiding this morning.

"What's up, Nellie?" I ask, approaching her locker during our passing period between first and second periods. "Have you seen Chance?" Mickey waddles her way down the main hall, trying to avoid sideswiping the other students rushing through the crowded hall. It's kind of hard to miss Mickey, though: big belly, braids, and all. I'm amazed she doesn't seem to feel self-conscious about being the only pregnant girl that we know of on campus. I would.

"No, I haven't, and I need to talk to him, pronto," Nellie says, switching out her history books and replacing them with her English texts. She slips the Louis Vuitton backpack onto her left shoulder and closes her locker door. When Nellie looks at me I notice her latest cosmetic addition. Not only did this girl dye her hair platinum blond, now she's got hazel contacts like the ones Mickey used to rock sometimes before her pregnancy. Mickey has opted for the simple life now because she says everything's too swollen to look too cute, including her eyeballs.

"Nellie, what's going on with those," I say, pointing at her new look. Mickey finally makes her way to her locker next to Nellie's, looking tired and out of breath. She's moving into the last few weeks of her pregnancy, and I know she's grateful because it's obviously wearing her ass out. Even if Mickey's still irritated with me about getting in good with Nigel's mom, I don't wish her any type of grief. I just wish my girls would get their heads straight, especially Nellie.

"I'm just trying something different," she says, looking at our friend open her locker. I guess she sees the same thing I do: a completely worn-down Mickey.

"Mickey, are you feeling okay?" Nellie asks, checking Mickey's forehead for a fever. Mickey jerks her head away from Nellie's touch. She shoots us both an evil glare.

"I'm fine, just pregnant," Mickey says, scratching her stomach like she's got fleas. She pulls her sweatshirt up and really goes at it.

"Problem?" I ask, leading us out of the main hall and into the language hall where my English class is housed. My girls also have English now, but their classroom is at the opposite end.

"Yes. These pants are annoying the hell out of me." Mickey's gray sweatpants are folded under her stomach, leaving her belly bare for all to see, and she couldn't care less. All she wants is to scratch her itchy skin, which doesn't seem to solve the problem.

"I don't think it's the pants," I say, reaching out and touching her newly forming stretch marks. As a perpetually skinny girl, Mickey has never known what it's like to gain and lose weight, or the inevitable growth marks that come with the transition. "It's your mama tattoos," I say, rubbing her stomach and connecting with my goddaughter, Nickey Shantae, who moves in recognition of my touch. I focus on her growing body, feeling her urge to get out, but it's not time yet. My mother's sight takes over my own vision, cooling both baby and mother down. Mickey stops scratching because I've soothed the itching for the moment.

"Don't they have some cocoa butter or something for that?" Nellie asks, looking at Mickey completely mortified. Being pregnant at any age is more than a notion, but in my opinion, no sixteen-year-old's body should be going through all of these changes. We've already got enough going on as teenagers without the added stress of growing a baby inside our bodies. I can only imagine what Mickey's going through, or so I think.

With my hands still on her bare abdomen, my fingers begin to tingle. I let go, surprised by the sensation, leaving Mickey's mind immediately. What the hell was that?

"It doesn't work," Mickey whines, almost in tears. "Nothing works. I can't sleep, I pee every fifteen minutes, and I've always got gas." Nellie and I look at each other, taking a step back in case our girl explodes in more ways than one.

"I can give you some of my grandmother's special belly balm, and I'm sure she has something to help your other issues, too," I say, wishing there was more I could do to help my friend, but Mickey has to go through this on her own. Mickey looks at me hopefully—not the disgusted look she usually gives when I suggest some of our homemade remedies.

"Bless you, Jayd," Mickey says, hugging me, which catches

me completely off guard. Mickey's not the affectionate type with anyone other than her man. I guess between the pregnancy and me chilling her out a bit, she's losing some of that tough, gangster girl exterior, and not a moment too soon. Mickey's baby is going to need all the tender loving care she can get.

The bell for second period rings loudly in our ears and lucky for me I'm not far from Mrs. Malone's class in the language hall adjacent to the main hall. My English teacher's been more lenient on her students than usual now that the AP exams are over. All we do in class these days is read and chat about our journal entries—no more exams or papers for the rest of the semester. We have one more short essay due, but it's on whatever topic we choose, based on our reading list for the year. We don't receive our summer reading list until the last week of school.

"I'll talk to y'all later," I say, heading toward my classroom. "And Nellie, when you see Chance, please tell him I need to talk to him about our scene before fifth period," I say. Nellie slits her multicolored fake eyes at me and then nods her head in agreement. This girl is too much for me. I'd better send Chance another text message myself rather than rely on Nellie to promptly deliver my message to her boyfriend. Sometimes her jealousy gets the best of her and that doesn't do any of us any good. If last night's dream weren't so urgent I would've never involved Nellie in my communication efforts, nor would I be so worried about my boy. But I know better than to ignore my dreams, especially when they're as lively as mine was last night.

"Settle down, class," Mrs. Malone says as we all file inside, ready to start the day. I guess Operation Find Chance will have to wait until break. Right now my time belongs to E. E. Cummings and Mrs. Malone. I'm actually enjoying reading his poetry. The cat's out there, but at least he's original with his shit, right down to the fact that he doesn't use capital letters in most of his writing. I like the white man's intellectual swag. It's the same type of confident genius Jeremy possesses. I can't wait to hug Jeremy up at break after I sign up for cheer. I missed seeing him this morning and I know he's still feeling tense after our run-in with Rah earlier this week. I've promised myself to be patient with Jeremy and let it flow because I like where we're headed.

It's break and I still can't believe I'm really doing this. I walk over to the long table where the cheerleaders are seated, taking my turn in line to sign up. I look around at the other dozen or so girls in line with me, noticing how excited most of them are. They look like they're freshmen, sophomores at most. I guess the juniors signed up earlier this week. There are three squads: freshman, junior varsity, and varsity, with the last two being based on ability more than grade level, but it's still an embarrassment for a senior to be placed on the JV squad, in sports and cheer.

"Hi," the perkier of the two black cheerleaders says to me, handing me a fluorescent flier and packet with all of the information necessary to apply. "My name is Shauna and I'm the captain of the varsity squad. This is Alicia, my cocaptain." Alicia's not as cheery as Shauna and I'm thankful for it. Maybe it's possible to be on the pep squad without being so damn peppy, which I equate with a white cheerleader's mode of operation. Perhaps Alicia's a real black girl after all; the jury's still out on Shauna.

"Hello, and welcome to the best week of your life," Alicia says, grinning from ear to ear as she reaches out her right hand for me to shake, showing her true cheerleader colors.

"Well, it's actually next week, but still, it begins today by you signing up." Shauna rises from her chair, smooths down her red and white pleated short skirt, and hands me the sign-up sheet and pen. Alicia looks at my hesitant stance, wondering if I'm going to actually do it, and the same question is running through my mind. Do I really want to do this?

Of course you do, my mom says, catching my drift. *Why not? You've got great legs, you can outperform any of those girls, and you've got sass. You'd make a perfect cheerleader, girl.*

But I already have a full plate, Mom, I think back, placing the packet down on the table and taking the clipboard from Shauna's hand, much to Alicia's approval. Maybe they need more allies on the squad, especially since she and the other sister will be graduating in a few weeks. I'm sure they don't want their black legacy to go. They're the only two girls on the large squad who have sass and spunk from what I've seen: the perfect combination for a good cheerleader.

Jayd, it'll be fun. And besides, you need to live a little. You're going into your senior year of high school and before you know it you'll be graduating. You deserve to have some fun while you still can. Before you know it, you'll be all grown up, and then you will have plenty of time to work—trust me. I know my mom's right. My mom was only nineteen when she had me, and that was the end of her fun for a while, if you let my mom tell it. I've been with my grandmother most of my life, and my mom's been making up for the time she lost in her first marriage ever since.

Fine. But when Mama gets pissed at me, I'm telling her you made me do it, I say from my mind to hers while simultaneously signing up for the tryouts. I can't believe I just did that.

It wouldn't be the first time and I'm sure it won't be the last, my mom says before finally leaving my thoughts. With my mom in my head I didn't have space to second-guess my actions for too long.

"Excellent!" Shauna exclaims, retrieving the clipboard and

checking off my name. "Please read over all of the information in the packet, sign your name where indicated, and come prepared for a good workout on Monday afternoon."

"You'll also need to have a copy of your transcripts and a one-paragraph statement on why you want to be on the pep squad. And dress in comfortable dance attire," Alicia says, all about the business without Shauna's enthusiasm.

"Rehearsals are for one hour after school every day next week, with tryouts the following week. We will post our decision on the gymnasium's announcement board next Friday." Shauna's all giggles as she puts a fresh sheet of notebook paper on the clipboard, ready for the next girl. There are a couple of guys on the squad, but they're usually off-season football players who want to get up the girls' skirts any way they can, including being the base of a human pyramid.

"Okay, thanks," I say, claiming my papers and leaving the line. On my way to third period I run into my man. It's the first time I've seen Jeremy this morning. This day and night surfing is wearing him out, but luckily the competition is next Saturday and then hopefully he'll be back to his mellow schedule.

"Hey, lady," Jeremy says, putting his right arm around my shoulders as I step into stride with him. He bends down, meeting my lips for a proper good morning hello.

"Hey, baby," I say, returning the affection as we head toward our government class. Mrs. Peterson's probably already there, with her perpetually grumpy ass. She's been more stoic than ever lately, only speaking to us to grunt out her orders for the day. I guess she's ready for summer to get here just like the rest of us.

"Did I just see you in the cheer line?" Jeremy asks. The idea still sounds so foreign. We never talked about it, but I think Jeremy's secretly hoping I don't become a member of the pep squad.

"Yes, you did, and before you say anything, yes, I really am."

Jeremy looks down at me like he doesn't recognize his girlfriend, but then softens his face into a smile. "Hey, I didn't say a word. And you know I'm down for you no matter what, Lady J," Jeremy says, taking my backpack from my right shoulder and carrying it to my desk. Who says chivalry is dead?

"I appreciate that, Mr. Weiner," I say, kissing him again before entering the grim room. It smells like Bengay and coffee in here, and it's colder than necessary if you ask me. "Have you spoken to Chance this morning?" I ask, taking my seat before Jeremy sits down next to me in our assigned row.

"No, and I called to check on him. I'm sure he's just taking a day off, but you wouldn't know anything about that now would you, Miss Jackson?" Jeremy's right. I never rest, but I don't feel like that's what's going on with our boy. I guess I'll have to do some extra footwork on this one myself. If Chance doesn't show up to Mr. Adewale's class next period, I'm going to take more drastic measures to share my dream with him. After all, his mother called me and I have to answer before it's too late.

Chance still hasn't returned any of my messages from this morning and because Jeremy and Nellie also haven't heard from him, I'm more worried than before. I took the liberty of asking Mrs. Sinclair if it was okay for me to be a little late to fifth period to see about her favorite student, and she was more than cool with it. I bet if it had been me in need, my ass would have been out of luck.

I pull up to Chance's mini Palos Verdes mansion and notice the flawless Chevy Nova parked in the driveway. The mere sight of the crimson classic makes my heart jump. It feels so good driving that thing, but that's not why I'm here.

I step out of my car and walk toward the house. It's too still around here for me. No matter how nice the neighborhood is, white folks have their fair share of family drama, too. I stopped by Taco Bell and grabbed Chance some lunch, mainly because I'm hungry and it is lunchtime. We both have to eat, and what better way to talk than by breaking tacos together?

I ring the doorbell on the massive oak-and-stained-glass front door. Without asking who it is, Chance opens the door looking like he just rolled out of bed.

"I decided to come and check on you since you can't return a sistah's calls and you decided to play hooky today," I say, stepping into the foyer and handing him his lunch. I can hear his mom on the phone in the living room and she doesn't sound happy.

"Yeah, sorry about that. I've had a lot on my mind," Chance says, closing the door behind us and smelling his lunch. He looks like he's been through hell and back. "Come on in," he says, ushering us into the dining room where we can eat and chill for a minute. We sit across from each other, both emptying the contents of our feast onto the marble table, ready to dig in. I can hear Mrs. Carmichael on the phone saying the words "help me" repeatedly, and feel the need to jump into Chance's mind to cool him off immediately. She's calling me again; only this time, instead of in my dream, I'm here to help my friend and his mother reconnect.

I jump into Chance's mind, seeing what he's not saying. He knows the entire truth about his birth mother's family, his adoption, his real name and all. He confronted his mother about his suspicions and she told him everything. It wasn't easy for either of them, but Chance feels betrayed by the woman he's loved as his mother his entire life. He wants to know why she didn't tell him the truth sooner and she can't explain her reasons to Chance, who is unyielding in his emotions. What a mess. At least I know my dreams are on point, as usual.

"Chance, what's really going on? You know you can tell me anything," I say, leaving his mind and focusing on opening the tiny hot sauce packets accompanying our meal. Chance picks up his burrito and takes a huge bite before letting it all out.

"I'm going to Georgia to see my real family, or at least the black side of it," Chance says proudly. I know it must feel like his mother kept this information from him for too long, but I know Mrs. Carmichael was just waiting for the right time to tell him. The worst part about that rationale is that there's no right time to tell someone they're adopted or that Chance's feelings of having black blood were valid. Somehow I have to get Chance to see that his mother's not his enemy.

"This is your real family," I say, gesturing at the large house around us. I know Mrs. Carmichael must be a total wreck, her only child leaving for Georgia and making her worst nightmare come true. From her psychic request, this is the best I can do on such short notice. I wish I could help more.

"I know my mom loves me, but all my life I've felt out of place at family reunions, the country club, summer camps where everyone was rich and white. I could never understand why, but now I know, Jayd. Now I know," Chance says, looking down at the blue paper in front of him and sliding it across the table for me to see. It's his birth certificate. Chase LeCroix Monroe. From my sleepwalk through his dream during the holidays, I remember that his mother is Creole and his daddy's a white boy, also from the South, whose family was adamantly against bringing home colored babies—but not mistresses—just like Jeremy's dad, who doesn't mind if

his son dates colored girls so long as they don't bring any
mixed babies home.

Mrs. Carmichael enters the room with a lit cigarette in one
hand and a glass of wine in the other, her cell phone propped
between her left ear and shoulder. She looks like hell, too.

"Hi, Mrs. Carmichael," I say, trying to hide my shock at her
tattered appearance. She really should consider cutting her
alcohol intake before the damage to her body is irreversible.

"Jayd, please talk some sense into this boy," his mother
says, completely beside herself. She looks like she's been crying for days. If I had to guess, I'd say she hasn't showered in
a couple of days, either.

"I already tried, but I think his mind's made up," I say, focusing on Mrs. Carmichael's eyes and jumping right into her
pain. It's so hot in here I'm starting to sweat. Calming her
down with my new powers is my biggest challenge yet. "You
should be as supportive as you can. You know Chance is your
baby, and he'll always come back to you." The tears stream
down Mrs. Carmichael's face and I've lost her. I should've
stopped while I was ahead because my last comment has
sent her into a complete frenzy.

"I gave you life, Chance Carmichael, do you hear me?
Even if I don't have the stretch marks to prove it, I'm still
your mother and you have to believe I would never do anything to intentionally hurt you. I love you, baby," Mrs.
Carmichael says, walking over to Chance and attempting to
hug him, but he refuses to let her get too close. She looks at
me hard before storming out of the dining room and up the
stairs. Damn, this is some heavy shit. I'm all for Chance finding out about his true lineage, but there's got to be a better
way to go about it.

"I called my mother's father and he says he's always wondered what happened to me. My mother's dead and he doesn't

know where my father is, but remembers a little about him," Chance says, choking back his tears. I see my boy's been busy playing detective the past couple of days. It's amazing how small the Internet makes the world. "I already got my plane tickets and packed my shit," Chance says, like it's no big deal. "I leave later this afternoon and will be back on Sunday."

"Is anyone going with you?" I ask after devouring the last of my chicken tacos. That was a slamming lunch even if the conversation wasn't as pleasant.

"No, and I don't want anyone to. This is something I have to do for myself." Chance takes another bite of his second burrito, avoiding my eyes. I really fear for my friend. He's suffering the loss of two mothers and doesn't know which to mourn first.

"I'm all about you finding your roots, but don't get it twisted, Chance. The grass isn't always greener. You don't know how your black side is going to respond to you. Are you sure you don't want your mom or Jeremy to go with you?" I would've offered my company, but Mama would never allow me to fly across country with one of my friends.

"I'm not sure about anything anymore, Jayd. I just want to get to Atlanta and see what my real mom looked like. If she had this mole on her lip like I do," he says, scratching his upper lip. "I always wondered where this damn thing came from." I hope Chance finds the answers he's looking for. It's not going to be easy, but life rarely is. I just hope he doesn't neglect Mrs. Carmichael's grief in the process. Her son's rightful search for self just might kill her.

"At least let me drive you to the airport. I got a school pass from Mrs. Sinclair and can take you whenever you're ready."

"I was born ready, Jayd. Let's roll," Chance says, rising from the table and jogging up the stairs two at a time to get his stuff. I can't believe he's going to Atlanta tonight. I'm glad Chance trusts me enough to be a part of his journey. After I drop him off I'll head straight to work, officially beginning my weekend. Like Chance, I hope I find some sort of peace over the next three days. God knows we both deserve it.

~ 4 ~
Ladies of Leisure

*"Never trouble no one/
I'm a lady, I'm not a man."*

—SISTER NANCY

Initially I'd hoped for a relaxing weekend, but it turned out to be the exact opposite, much to my bank account's benefit. I had clients stacked up at the shop and at my mom's apartment. As if doing hair all weekend wasn't enough, I also had spirit work and my boyfriend to keep me busy, not to mention studying the sorority's history for the debutante meeting at Mrs. Esop's house later this afternoon. I'm as ready as I'll ever be to deal with the ladies of leisure Mrs. Esop associates with. Tolerating their bougie asses will be a challenge, but nothing I can't stomach for a couple of hours.

After braiding all morning, I came over to Mama's to help her fill some of her special Mother's Day orders for next Sunday's holiday, which also happens to be Mama's favorite day of the year after Christmas, and have been working in the spirit room ever since. She and Netta get all dressed up and go out after their all-day ritual honoring our ancestral mothers. It's a beautiful ceremony and I always feel renewed after participating every year.

I have yet to tell Mama about me becoming a debutante with Mrs. Esop's sorority and possibly a cheerleader next year. Much like with my Advanced Placement exams, Mama won't be happy with the time spent on my newfound extracurricular activities. I don't know how to break the news to her, but it has to be done. I'm sure she's going to wonder why I can't stay for dinner today, and lying about it won't work with Mama for long. It's going to be a tough sell, though. She's never gotten along well with Nigel's mother, who thinks my grandmother is related to the Antichrist and Mama feels the same way about her. Their hating goes back to when Mrs. Esop was still in Compton, having come from Louisiana with Mama, Netta, Esmeralda and a lot of our other neighbors. I wonder if Mrs. Esop's snooty friends feel the same way. If they say one cross word about my grandmother or my mother, I'm out—damn our verbal agreement.

"Jayd, hand me the shea butter, please. And could you crush some more vanilla beans for the big belly balm? We're going to need it for that girl's growing stomach," Mama says, mixing the ingredients in the mortar. I'm so glad she's making a special batch of the cream for Mickey, even though Mama made it very clear it's for the baby and not my fast-ass friend.

"What does vanilla do besides make it smell good?" I ask, immediately sorry that I did. I take the small, dark brown beans out of one of the dozens of glass containers lining the shelves. The look in Mama's eyes is enough to show how much she's disappointed in my lack of spiritual prowess. I've been studying my spirit lessons, but not as much as she thinks I should. I can't tell her that I'm more interested in studying about my mom's gift of sight than about ingredients for the various recipes Mama specializes in. After a few more minutes, Mama softens her look and answers my question.

"Vanilla has many benefits. For expectant mothers it is a soothing herb, especially when coupled with sandalwood and lavender," she says, taking more of the ground ingredi-

ents from the cutting board and drizzling them into a marble
bowl before beating them with the matching pestle. I love
Mama's tools. She rarely lets me use the ancient bowl and
pounder because she's afraid I'll break them. But the various
wooden combinations lining the cabinets work just as well
for me.

"The balm smells so good I could spread it on a biscuit
and eat it," I say, mixing the almond oil, melted cocoa butter,
and another special oil Mama didn't give me the name of, in
my smaller mortar, waiting for further instructions.

"You could, but it might not taste so good," Mama says,
smiling at me. It's always nice being in the spirit room with
Mama, especially when it's a bright, sunny day like today. It's
over eighty degrees outside and a slight breeze is blowing
through the screen door, dispersing our healing scents through
the tiny house. Even Lexi—Mama's loyal German shepherd—
is enjoying the day from her usual post at the threshold.
"Which reminds me, what are we having for dinner this evening? I've got some fresh salmon from Mr. Webb and we can
make some honey butter and biscuits to go with it." Oh, that
sounds so delicious. I know they won't have anything like
that to eat at the tea this afternoon.

"About that," I say, easing into my admission. "I actually
have a function to attend this afternoon and I don't think I'll
make it back in time for dinner." Mama continues her mixing, not looking up from the smooth concoction. I hope
Mickey knows what she's getting, but she probably doesn't
and couldn't care less about the spiritual relevance of having
a priestess like Mama making her something to smooth her
stretch marks and many other ailments she may experience.

"I see," she says, finally done with the balm. I automatically claim an empty plastic container from the counter and
hand it to Mama to fill. I busy myself with the label making

while the thought of me not being here for our now regular Sunday dinner sets in, filling the room with an uncomfortable silence.

"I've been meaning to talk to you about something," I say, taking Mickey's full container and pressing the label onto the front. I then walk over to the ancestor shrine and place the balm next to the rest of the products lined up for blessings. This is the final ingredient that makes Mama's line of healing and beauty products so special and powerful. Once she prays over them, they're ready to go. "I've been invited by Nigel's mother to participate in a debutante ball."

"A debutante ball—by Nigel's mother," Mama repeats, rubbing the remnants of the balm into her already glistening skin. "And you accepted the invitation, I assume." I stare at Mama, who's focused on her hands. She can tell there's more I'm not saying.

"Yes, I did, but only because Mrs. Esop made me agree to it in exchange for her presence at Mickey's baby shower, where she only came downstairs to say hello. But in her eyes, her part of the deal was met, so I have to keep my word, too." I join Mama at the kitchen table, sitting on a stool across from her. Her green eyes look weary and I wonder if she's been taking her herbs regularly since I moved out. I'd never forgive myself if something happened to Mama because I don't live here anymore.

"Yes, you must keep your word," she says cryptically. Mama looks behind her at the refrigerator and claims the spirit book from the top. "And?" Mama asks, waiting for the rest of my confession. This must be how it feels to let it all out to a Catholic priest.

"And all next week I'll be an hour late to Netta's because I'm trying out for the cheer squad. My counselor, Mr. Adelizi, says it will help my chances of getting into a good college."

Mama looks up at me, shocked by that last bomb. "I know, I know, it's not my thing, but he says that I need another activity to make me a solid candidate."

"Mrs. Esop, Mr. Adelizi. Who the hell are these people to you, Jayd?" Mama taps her long, red fingernail on the book three times before opening it to exactly what she was looking for, I suppose. That's just how gifted Mama is. The book speaks to her, unlike when I ask it a question. I have to look through the entire thing to find what I'm looking for. I wonder if there's a silent prayer or something that comes along with the nail tapping that I need to become privy to.

"Well, Mr. Adelizi is my guidance counselor at school and, well, you know who Mrs. Esop is," I say, realizing how silly I must sound. Mama bends her neck to the right and opens her mouth in total disbelief that I had the nerve to answer her rhetorical question.

"Jayd, I have tolerated your recent shenanigans as best I know how. But, girl, I think you're really losing it." Mama closes her eyes and scratches her forehead like she's completely stressed, and I feel her. I hardly recognize myself sometimes, but I feel like the same person. What gives?

"Mama, it's not that bad. I'm just growing up, I guess."

"Growing up means maturing, not completely changing who you are at the influence of outsiders." Mama opens her eyes and silently reads a few lines from the great book.

"Outsiders?" I say aloud, questioning the word's use in this case. I know what Mama means, but I see these people on a regular basis.

"Yes, Jayd. Outsiders: people who are not a part of your family, your lineage, your bloodline. Your destiny was carved out way before you were even thought of, little girl. And the path you're etching out for yourself is in direct contradiction to that divine destiny." Mama continues her reading, taking one of the loose note cards from the ancient text and using it as a bookmark. Unlike the pages in this book, my life's not written yet.

"Don't I get a say in the way my life unfolds?" I know I sound like a bratty teenager but for real. I've been living this spiritual life for seventeen years now. When do I get a break to just do me? I know my life includes the crazy dreams and everything else that comes with my lineage, and I've accepted that. But there has to be a way to balance the best of both worlds. Otherwise, what's the point?

"Of course you do, just like your mama did. And we see how well that turned out," Mama says, eyeing the weathered pages in front of her. I don't like where this conversation is leading and from the look of it, neither does my grandmother.

"But my mom turned out okay in the end," I say, fingering the five jade bracelets on my left arm. I wonder if they can protect me against the wrath I feel coming from Mama.

"Yes, she did. And as her mother, I'm just grateful she's alive and healthy—for the most part."

"What do you mean, 'for the most part'? Is there something I should know?" I ask, alarmed at the possibility my mother's ill or something else just as disturbing.

"Nothing that you aren't already aware of," Mama says, rubbing her tired eyes underneath her reading glasses. "For a priestess to lose her power is tantamount to one losing a hand or the use of their eyes. So like I said, Lynn Marie is healthy, for the most part."

"I don't see what me getting involved in more school activities has to do with my sight. I'm still dreaming and retaining my memory, just like I'm supposed to," I say, stopping short of admitting I've retained more than a memory from one of my dreams about my mother. I'm still in disbelief that

I've kept her powers, but I'm not letting Mama know or she'll strip me of them before I can make a good case as to why I should keep them. They've already been beneficial to my friends and Mrs. Carmichael, and that has to count for something.

"Yes, about that," Mama says, turning the book around to face me. "You have no idea what you're supposed to be able to do because you don't spend enough time on your spirit studies. How do you know what your true potential is if you don't invest fully in your talent?"

"Exactly my point about cheer and becoming a debutante," I say, surprised at the logic in my argument. Why am I so gung ho about making a case for my newfound activities when I myself am fundamentally against becoming active in either group? I guess now that they're on the table I feel like I want to keep them, just like my mom's cold-ass abilities and my bid for ASU president. They're both in my destiny and it's time to claim them.

"Jayd, what the hell good is becoming a debutante going to do you? Those heffas know nothing about real work or our way of life. All they do is sip tea and talk shit," Mama says, shuddering at the thought. "Trust me, Jayd, I know more about that world than you realize. Me and Teresa go way, way back and despite her name, she's no saint." I've never heard Mama refer to Nigel's mother by her first name. I almost forgot she had one.

"I know she's a tough lady, but this opportunity is bigger than her. Besides, I gave my word." I look at the wall clock and realize it's already past noon. I need to do my hair, raid what's left of my mother's clothes for something suitable to wear to the tea, and get a move on. I'm a bit nervous about meeting the ladies of leisure, as Nigel calls his mom's sorority sisters, but I'm also excited. It's nice being chosen, even if

I wasn't running for anything. Speaking of which, I also have to write my speech for the election during the African Student Union meeting on Wednesday at lunch. I've made a good case for myself and think I'm a shoo-in for president, but one can never be too sure.

"Be careful about spreading your word too thin, Jayd. Just like your ass, it can get worn out." Mama places the last index card in the spirit book and pushes it across the table toward me. "Here's your lesson for the week. Study it well. There will be a test at Netta's soon." Mama rises from her stool, walks over to me and kisses me long on the forehead. "I love you, baby. Have a good time at your tea."

"Thank you, Mama. I love you, too." I hug her tightly before she exits the small house with Lexi at her heels.

The section Mama has chosen for this week's lesson, is all about verbal ashe, or the spoken word. This should be an interesting lesson to say the least. I have about an hour before I have to get going. I'll read as much as I can and take notes to study later. The rest will have to be done tomorrow after work. I don't have much time to get ready, hair included. Balancing my new priorities with my old ones will take some serious juggling. Hopefully, I'll get better at it because I can't keep neglecting my spirit work or Mama.

When I made it back to my mom's place a couple of hours ago, I took a quick shower and touched up my hair before raiding my mom's dwindling wardrobe. Slowly but surely my mom's things are making their way over to her boyfriend's apartment, undoubtedly forcing some of his stuff out. I finally settled on a cream silk skirt suit with a pink shell underneath and pink snakeskin pumps to match. I look so good I wish I had somewhere else to show off my sophisticated clothes. If I don't look like a lady, then I don't know who does. We'll see if Nigel's mother and her friends agree. I send Jeremy a quick text to let him know I'm thinking about my boo. He's probably in the deep blue sea riding a wave, or whatever it is they do at the beach all day. Maybe we can meet up tonight after we're done with both of our busy days.

Not fully realizing what I was getting myself into when I arrived at Nigel's house twenty minutes ago, I walked into his foyer greeted by thirty or so girls my age and other women in the sorority. I had no idea there would be so many people here, all wondering who I am and where the hell I came from, causing me to feel like an outsider in a house I chill at on the regular. I may look as nice as the other young ladies present, but there's something about the way people with money walk that I don't possess. These broads are sizing me up and I'm doing the same thing to them. Now that we've all served ourselves tea and cookies, we're seated in the living room ready to get started.

"Good afternoon, ladies," Mrs. Esop says, gently tapping the side of the petite china teacup she's holding with an equally dainty silver spoon, officially calling the meeting to order. "We, the lovely ladies of Alpha Delta Rho, would like to welcome you to our first debutante tea, one of many mandatory social gatherings you'll participate in over the next several weeks." She places the cup on the coffee table across from where she's seated on the couch, allowing another elder to continue.

"I'm Mrs. Tyler, vice president of our chapter, and you've just heard from our president, Mrs. Esop," she says, smoothing the cloth napkin over her lap before taking a sip of her tea. "Because this is our first tea, we are going to take this opportunity to get to know each of you on a more friendly basis. So mingle and take in some of the lovely art on the walls. We'll hold the history quiz after we get to know one another better." Mrs. Tyler and Mrs. Esop join the rest of the women walking around the large room, checking out us girls. They seem to be watching our social etiquette. I think I'll just stay where I am and let the wolves come to me. "So you must be the infamous Jayd," Mrs. Tyler says, sizing me up. "My soror here has told me a lot about you," she says, gesturing with her teacup toward Nigel's mom, who's standing beside her. Unlike the white women in PV, these black elitists don't drink alcohol during the day out of fear of being deemed uncivilized. Too bad, because they could really use some loosening up in here.

"Jayd Jackson, Lynn Mae James's granddaughter?" one of the other women asks, suddenly interested, in the small section of the room where I'm now cornered by these three ladies. "Hello, dear. I'm Mrs. Pierce, social secretary." Here we go.

"Yes ma'am, I am," I answer, trying to remain polite as my blood pressure rises. I don't want to have to cuss anyone out today, but if she says one wrong word about my grandmother, it's going to be on and cracking in Lafayette Square, tea be damned.

"How is our soror?" Mrs. Tyler asks, catching me completely off guard. Soror? Mama's not a member of their sorority, is she? I know Mrs. Esop is closer to Mama's age than my mom's, being that Mrs. Esop's eldest child is several years older than Nigel, but I'm not sure exactly how old she is.

"Now, Rita, you know Lynn Mae left us a long, long time ago." Mrs. Esop winks at me as she puts the tea tray down on the coffee table. "As a matter of fact, she was never really with us."

"Yet and still, her daughter's wearing our colors. Go figure," Mrs. Pierce says, looking at my pink shoes and shell, smiling at my chosen attire.

"*Granddaughter*—and she's only wearing half of them, or

have you forgotten how well crimson goes with pink?" Mrs.
Esop asks, visibly annoyed by her friend's reference, but I'm
not too sure which one. The way she said *granddaughter*
was like she wanted to make sure the separation was clear
between generations. And as for the colors, I think all Greek
organizations are just one step away from being as devoted
to their colors as gangs are, yet they strive to be seen as the
exact opposite. Go figure.

"Yes, dear. And when's the last time you wore the two together?" Mrs. Tyler asks while helping herself to the efferves-
cent drink in her hand. Maybe there's a little something extra
in her cup.

"I love my ladies, but really, pink and red just don't mix,"
Mrs. Pierce says, touching up her tea with the small kettle on
the side table next to my chair. There are a variety of teas in
the ceramic bowls on the coffee table, as well as flavored instant coffees, Mama's favorite. The three women are standing
over me, dominating my space and the conversation. One of
the younger sisters decides to take the initiative and join our
side chat.

"What about Valentine's Day? They are the two main colors, and I think they look lovely together," she says, but I
think that was the wrong thing to say because the elder sisters look at her like she has horns sticking out of her head. At
least her comment got me out of the hot seat.

"Natalia, only speak when spoken to, understood?" Mrs.
Tyler says, seemingly embarrassed for the young woman.
"Jayd, this is my daughter Natalia. She's so excited to be here."

"Hello," I say, reaching out my hand for the tall, slender
sister to take. She looks at my hand, hesitating before touching my fingers.

"Charmed, I'm sure." I look up at the broad, feeling the
need to stand up so she doesn't get it twisted. Just because
I'm new to this socialite bull doesn't mean I'm lower than

anyone else. Before I can get too caught up in the Japanese animation flick in my head—me wiping the floor with Natalia's Gucci sundress—Mrs. Esop interjects, calling the room back to order.

"Young ladies," Mrs. Esop says, commanding our attention. She is definitely the baddest broad in here and her sisters seem to know it. I guess that's why she's president. I hope I command the same respect when I win the ASU race. "We are going to begin the interview process now. Please step into the dining room and we'll come get you individually when your time comes. There are more pastries and drinks in there to enjoy." The fifteen of us leave the large space, leaving our sponsors in the living room, and walk toward the dining room, everyone paired up but me. There are fifteen of us and because it's an odd number, someone's going to be left out. I let them go into the quaint space, chitchatting it up while I head through the kitchen and toward the front door. I need some air.

"Jayd, is that you?" Nellie asks. Mickey comes in the front door behind her. I guess my friends are having a session during our teatime. Good. Maybe I can kick it after I'm done here.

"The one and only," I say, smiling at them both. Even if we're on weird terms, I'm still happy to see familiar faces.

"Out of my way, please. I have to pee," Mickey says, passing me by on her way to the guest bathroom in the hallway. I'm glad I have Mickey's balm in the car. Chance and Nigel are walking up the driveway carrying the bags from this afternoon's shopping trip.

"Wow," Chance says, hugging me, careful not to wrinkle my mom's suit. "You clean up well, boo." Nellie hits him on the arm, but it's no use. Chance and I will always be cool like that. I guess he just got back from Atlanta. We'll have to talk about his trip later since he asked me to keep his family secret on the low. I know Nellie's going to be pissed when she finds out Chance confided in me and not her, but I think Chance needed to trust this newfound development in his life with a longtime friend, not his new and unpredictable narcissistic girlfriend. I totally get it, but I doubt Nellie will be as understanding.

Nigel comes up the porch steps, seeing the same thing they all see: a new Jayd. Damn, do I really look that different?

"Well, well, well. They've got you now, don't they?" Nigel says, hugging me and kissing me on the cheek. "You look good, girl."

"Yeah, Jayd. We almost didn't recognize you," Nellie says, and I don't think that was a compliment. "We'd better get this stuff upstairs," Nellie says, leading the way out of the foyer and through the hallway toward the staircase. Nigel and Chance follow her as Mickey makes her way out of the bathroom.

"By the way, Jayd. Rah says holla at him when you get a min." Nigel waits for Mickey to pass and then walks behind her.

"Oh, and Jayd," Chance says, turning around in midstep and stopping their trek before leaving the hall. "My mom wants to know if you could come to dinner soon." Nellie looks back at me, wearing a scowl like I just slapped her in the face. Chance could have saved that invite for later, but I don't think he sees the harm in always being truthful about his shit. He'd better learn self-censorship and soon if he's going to have a girl like Nellie on his arm.

"Hi, kids. Jayd, we're ready for you," Mrs. Esop says, stepping into the foyer and greeting my friends walking up the stairs. I watch them disappear upstairs as I return to my fate, down here. I don't know that I'm making the right decision, but I'm here now and I have to walk my chosen path to see where it leads me. I'll worry about the rest tomorrow.

* * *

After the end of a very long afternoon yesterday, I joined my crew upstairs and chillaxed with them for the rest of the evening. I gave Mickey her balm and she used it immediately. After getting instant relief, she was too relaxed to be irritated with me anymore, but Nellie's another story. I haven't run into either one of my girls this morning, but it's still early in the day.

"Jayd, how come you didn't tell me about the auditions for the spring play and that you're not trying out for the lead?" Ms. Toni asks, approaching my locker with a handful of files. "Since when don't you want to be the star you were born to be?" No hi, hello—nothing. Just straight to the point, as usual. I love my school mama, but sometimes I just need a hug, not a tongue-lashing.

"It's complicated," I say, closing my locker door and facing Ms. Toni. I hug her tall, slender frame and walk with her toward her office a few feet away in the middle of the large hall. I wish she'd stop smoking. I can smell it all over her soft black sweater. Perhaps there's something in the spirit book that'll give her just the push she needs to get rid of the cigarettes once and for all. Maybe she'll even let me do her hair, too.

"Jayd, didn't the last time you got in trouble with Mrs. Bennett—after Laura mysteriously lost her voice during the fall play—teach you not to keep secrets from me? I can't help you if we don't have full disclosure." Ms. Toni and I almost fell out permanently over my role in that one.

"That's just it, Ms. Toni. I don't need help this time because I know exactly what I should do. And in this case, that's trying out for the supporting role." Ms. Toni wants me to confide in her about everything, including my spirit drama, but I can't.

"You owe it to yourself and every other little black girl after you to try out and win this part. You know these white folks up here will take your retreat as their personal win if you don't, girl. They already are. You should hear Laura and Mrs. Bennett praising themselves." Damn, do I always have to be the spokesperson for the successful black child up here? I'm tired of wearing that crown.

"I'm already running for ASU president and trying out for cheer, not to mention my life outside of school. I'm tired, Ms. Toni," I say, realizing I'm whining. I wave at Maggie and her Latino crew coming into the hall from the other end, envying their chill existence. How come Ms. Toni's not all up in her ass to become the first Latina to do all the great things she's always putting me up to?

"Stop complaining and handle your business, little girl," Ms. Toni says, patting me on the shoulder before retreating to her office. Her and her drive-bys.

Ms. Toni's right. I owe it to myself and the other black students interested in drama to audition for the lead role. Besides, I can always step down if playing a blind woman proves to be too much for me. Winning the part will be victory enough for me, and that starts with trying out for the right part this afternoon.

I'd think that my friends would want to start the week off at school, but no such thing. Nigel, Nellie, Jeremy, and Mickey are all missing today, making it a very quiet Monday. I heard from my man at break when he texted me good morning. Jeremy was just waking up and decided to stay at home for the rest of the day. I know Chance will be here for the auditions in class this period, but the rest of my crew I haven't heard from.

"Welcome to the next round of auditions for the spring

play, *Wait Until Dark,*" Mrs. Sinclair announces, hushing the
vibrant room. We've all been rehearsing our monologues
since class began, and I can't wait to get this over with. Luckily, we can read from the script for auditions and I had to
read Susy's lines to study for Gloria since most of their
scenes are together. I'm really uncomfortable playing the
role of a blind woman, but I can't miss the opportunity to audition for the lead in the last play of the year, especially after
the grilling Ms. Toni gave me earlier this afternoon, and she's
right to some extent. But the bottom line is, I have to trust
my ashe, and as Mama says, if it doesn't feel good I won't do
it. But I still owe it to myself to try.

"Today we will do a test run for the main characters Mike,
Carlino, Roat, Susy, Sam, and Gloria." Everyone looks
through their scripts, marking the pages where the names
are present, ready to read. I look through my pages, carefully
eyeing Susy's lines. I do like her spunk, although Gloria's not
bad either—for a little girl. But Susy's the strong, savvy one
and I think I'd make a great leading lady.

"I'm a shoo-in for Carlino," Chance says, reveling in playing one of the bad guys. He was only in Atlanta for three days
and already has a different swag about him.

"Why not Mike?" I ask, reading through the opening scene
where the crooks are trying to figure out what's going on.
They're all in money trouble and need to find the doll filled
with heroin, which is where Sam, Susy, and Gloria come in.

"Because he's not a leader like I am, you know what I'm
saying?"

"Yeah, I know what you're saying." I look at my friend, recognizing the change in his physical appearance and overall
demeanor since finding out he's got a little black in him.
Chance is growing more comfortable with himself. How can
I hate on him for that? I hope his dad and girlfriend are also

adjusting to this newfound attitude of his. I don't know about the name change, but Mama always taught me that there's a lot of power in what we call ourselves. And if Chance wants to be called by his birth name, Chase, I'm all for it.

"All right, which group is up first?" Mrs. Sinclair asks, waiting for volunteers from the class. We might as well get it over with, especially since we missed the first read-through Friday afternoon. Before I can get up from my seat, Laura and Reid— the self-proclaimed king and queen of ASB—walk into the auditions. I hope she's not considering trying out for the role. Alia and I walk onto the floor with Chance and Seth right behind us. Emilio's also here, ready to try out. I hate that auditions have to be open to everyone. You never know who's going to come in and ruin the vibe we thespians have got going on in here.

"Okay, it looks like we have readers for each part," Mrs. Sinclair says, giving Matt the cue to lower the lights, hushing the bustling room. "Let's begin. Scene one." Alia and I step out of the center, allowing the guys to show off for the first part of the scene. Then Alia and I dominate the second scene, she reading for Gloria and I for Susy. After it's over, the class gives our group a standing ovation and we know we deserve it.

"You looked good out there," Alia says, hugging me tightly, and I return the affection. She's always been cool with me.

"So did you. I think you're selling yourself short trying out for Gloria," I say, fanning myself with the script in my hand. The spotlights always feel like heat lamps beaming on my head. It was scary for a moment there when the lights blinded me, but I don't think that was a coincidence. Maybe if I can convince Alia to try out for the lead in the next round, I can try out for Gloria. I wouldn't mind losing the part to

her, but to Laura—never again. When she conned her way
into the female lead for *Macbeth,* with Misty and Esmeralda's
help, I had to snatch it back from her by using a special spray
that made her lose her voice on opening night, handing the
crown back to me, its rightful owner. This time I won't have
to go through all of that because she's not even going to be
in the running if I can help it.

"You know that part is yours, Jayd. You were on fire out
there," Alia says, giving me another big hug. If she only knew
how truthful that statement really is.

"Let's make a deal. If we both get the parts we auditioned
for, we'll be each other's understudies. Deal?"

"It's a deal, Jayd," Alia says, eyeing Chance talking to Matt
beside us. She obviously has it bad for my boy. I wonder if
Chance knows he has a not-so-secret admirer.

"Well done," Laura says to Alia, who smiles big at the compliment. I know better than to take anything this heffa says at
face value. Laura looks down at me, her skinny, tall frame reminding me of Olive Oyl from *Popeye,* and smiles. What's she
up to now?

"Jayd, are you ready? We need to rehearse our lines for the
second round tomorrow," Chance asks, trying to save me before my head gets hot again. He knows I can't stand Reid and
Laura for any longer than I have to. It's bad enough I have
classes with them on my AP track, but now that I'm trying out
for cheer, if I make the squad I will no doubt have to be involved in certain ASB activities shared with the athletes and
cheerleaders crew. What a compromise I'm making to get
into a good college. I just hope it's all worth it in the end.

Before I can escape, Laura opens her mouth, forcing me
to listen.

"Jayd, you have read the script, right?" Laura asks. Why is
this broad begging me to slap her, and in public, too?

"Yes, Laura. In case you haven't noticed, this is a classroom and we are real students." Drama class gets a bad rap for being an easy elective when it's anything but. Mrs. Sinclair is serious about her students knowing the ins and outs of all our productions, and that includes reading the back stories on all scripts as well as the full plays themselves.

"Well, in that case, I'm sure you've noticed that Susy is a tall, sophisticated woman living in New York and that you, of course, don't fit that description, no matter how good of an actress you assume yourself to be." Alia and Chance look at each other and back at Laura, shocked by her bold ignorance. Who the hell does this heffa think she is, walking into our class and deciding who fits the bill and who doesn't? What she really stops short of saying is that I'm a short black girl from Compton and shouldn't even consider auditioning for the part.

"What's your problem, Laura?" Chance asks before the words can escape my mouth. That's my boy, slamming her when I can't. Chance always has my back. I'm trying to keep myself from cussing her out, but I don't know if I can think of another more appropriate response to her inquiry. Laura's a bitch and then some. And ever since Nellie started hanging out with her, she's becoming more and more like Laura every day.

"The auditions are open to anyone who wants to try out, regardless of how they look or whether or not they can act," Alia says, visibly uncomfortable with Laura's point of view.

"Yes, but let's be real. This part is not made for you, Jayd," Laura says, reminding me of Bree's stuck-up ass from *Desperate Housewives*. I'm about to get like Gabrielle and tell her tall, white ass off. "Why don't you try out for something more suitable? Maybe next year there'll be more options for someone like you." That's it. The bitch is getting slapped down to the floor and now.

"Laura, why do you always want to start some shit with

me?" I ask, stepping up to Laura, who stops smiling at my approach. "I've never caused you or little man any trouble, but for some reason you two are always hating on me. Am I that much of a threat to your happy, white world?" Reid looks dead in my eyes like he knows I won't give him a psychic beat-down with my great-grandmother, Maman's, gift of sight like I did a couple of months ago when I initiated the African Student Union at South Bay, much to his disliking. These are two of the most covertly racist and obviously snobbish teenagers I've ever met. If the saying about the fruit not falling too far from the tree is true, I'd hate to run into their parents.

"You're no threat at all, Jayd. Quite to the contrary, actually," Reid says, taking his tall broad by the waist and stepping fully into our edgy cipher. The rest of the class prepares for the bell that's about to ring and I should be right there with them, considering my sixth period weight lifting class is all the way across campus. But instead I'm dealing with this bull. What the hell? "We're just trying to save you from the embarrassment, Jayd. Let's just say that you do win the part. No one wants to see you play the lead, and therefore no one will come to opening night." What universe do they live in?

"Are you on crack, man? Because you know you don't have to actually deal with drugs to audition for one of the dudes, right?" Chance asks, bringing some comedy into his insult, as always. "In case you forgot, the fall play was sold out every night, and Jayd was leading lady then and will be this time, too." Noticing the tension, Mrs. Sinclair makes her way over to us, ready to accuse me, as always, of starting some shit.

"Jayd, what's going on here?" See what I'm saying? Why does it always have to be my fault when shit's foul?

"I don't know. You'll have to ask them, and I need to get

to class," I say, pointing at Reid and Laura before excusing myself from the dramatic side scene not written in the script. "Later, y'all." I don't have time this afternoon. How one of my best friends could be cool with those bigots is beyond me. And I'm always the one accused of stabbing folks in the back. As if.

~ 5 ~
Backstabber

"Hit the road, Jack/
And don't you come back no more."

—RAY CHARLES

"*Jayd, watch where you're going!*" *Mama shouts at me from a distance, but I can't see a damned thing in the thick mist surrounding me. Is it day or night? Are we outside or in? I can't tell anything, and because my vision is limited, the rest of my senses are way off. Unlike when other folks lose one of their senses, ours are not compensated when we lose our gift of sight, leaving us extremely vulnerable to our surroundings—including the people around us.*

"She gave it up too soon," another voice says. It sounds like Maman, Mama's mother, but I can't tell. I seem to be losing my hearing, too. I've got to snap out of this dream and fast, before I lose all of my senses.

Walking like a blind woman through a minefield, I put my hands out in front of me, feeling for any possible obstructions in my path. What happened to my eyes and why am I walking by myself? Where's my mother? Where's Mama? Suddenly I feel a hand on my left shoulder, causing me to stop in my tracks.

"Jayd, you need to get out of here, now," the unfamiliar voice says, turning me around in the opposite direction. How do I know I can trust this person when I can't even tell who it is? I touch the hand on my shoulder, feeling for the

arm it should be connected to. Before I can scream, I feel Mama's presence enter the space and the lone hand disappears.

"No, Jayd. Turn around. It's the wrong way, girl," I hear Mama say, but it's too late. I'm already gone, and the farther I walk, the more distant Mama's voice becomes. For some reason I am drawn toward the strong gust of wind I'm walking against. The hand on my shoulder returns, pushing me forward, and I continue my trek toward I-don't-know-where. The farther I walk, the colder and stronger the wind gets, but I'm determined to arrive at my mystery destination.

"Jayd, please turn around and go back. You don't know what you're getting yourself into," says a voice that sounds like a whisper of my mom's sweet voice in my ear. "Please don't do this." I hear her, but I can't stop now. I've come too far to not see where this road leads. The hand on my shoulder gently squeezes, signaling for me to stop where I am. Now completely blind, I wave my hands frantically in front of me, reaching for anything that might serve as a clue to where I am, but I've got nothing.

"We're here," the voice says, now raspier than before. She sounds like an evil witch, and the fear of the unknown sets in. What the hell have I done? And why didn't I listen to my mothers when I surely knew better? Even my sense of reasoning is lost when I can't see.

"I want to go back," I say, turning around, but the hand touches me again, this time more forcefully, turning me back around. I can't hear a thing now and wish I had listened to my elders before. Even if their voices sounded different, I should've trusted them.

"Not a chance," the frigid voice says, urging me forward. "You're here now and you belong to us." Tears fall down my cheeks, reminding me of the time I was blinded while reliv-

ing the day my mom lost her powers and how horrible it felt to be robbed of my sight. What if I never get out of this dream? I remember my lessons from a couple of nights ago, which spoke about the power of the mind even when unconscious. Let's see if I can will myself out of this nightmare.

"You can't make me stay if don't want to," I say, grabbing the cold hand and removing it from my body. Once free, I start to run in the opposite direction, but because I can't see a thing, I have no idea where I'm running to or whom I'm running from. I just know I need to move.

The hand again reclaims my shoulder, now hurting me to the point of paralysis. What is this, some kung fu shit? She again turns me around in the opposite direction, pushing me quickly forward and then stopping. I turn around again and push back as hard as I can, forcing her hand free and running again, but now it's a steep hill I have to climb. I can't hear her creep up behind me as she grabs me by the ankles, dragging me back down.

"You can't run from me, little Jayd." Now it's clear whom the voice belongs to: Esmeralda. How did she get into my dreams again? And how can I get away from her, permanently?

"There's only one way to get away from me," Esmeralda says, answering my unspoken question. Pulling me to my feet, we're right back where we started. The wind is too powerful for me to try running again. All I can do is hold my ground and pray that I wake up soon. "And I'll gladly grant your wish." Before I can protest, Esmeralda stabs me in the back with something sharp and I fall forward off of what feels like a cliff. Oh hell no. Why is this bitch always trying to kill me?

"Ahhh!" I scream, waking a sleeping Jeremy and probably the rest of my mom's neighborhood. I bet Mama even heard me all the way in Compton. I grab my throat, touch my ears and then wave my hands in front of my face, checking my senses to make sure they're all good.

"Jayd, what's wrong?" Jeremy asks, leaping to his feet and turning on the lamp. He sits back down on the living room floor and holds me tightly. I look around the apartment, thankful for my vision. "Are you okay, baby?" I'm not really sure, but I don't want to scare him any more than I already have.

"Yes. It was just a bad dream," I say, wiping the tears from my cheeks. I know Jeremy doesn't understand what I go through as a voodoo priestess on the regular, but at least he's compassionate.

"That was one hell of a dream to make you cry," he says, leaning up against the wall next to our makeshift cot. He lifts my chin and looks into my eyes, wiping the remaining tears away. I wish the memory of my nightmare could fade as easily. I try to shake the image of being blind out of my head, but it's no use.

"Yeah, it was." I don't want to relive the details right now and I hope Jeremy doesn't pry. I glance at the clock on the DVD player and we only have two more hours to sleep before our school day begins. Maybe I can fall back into a sweet dream to make up for that frightening shit. Jeremy hugs me tightly, rubbing my back and kissing my forehead. I can tell he's worried. This is one of those times I wish Mama were here to comfort me, but my man's doing his best to calm my jittery nerves.

"I'm sorry, baby. You don't have to be afraid. I'm right here," Jeremy says, lying back down with me on his chest and pulling the blankets over us both. He's such a good boyfriend. Jeremy's been extra tired, surfing until dark in preparation for his upcoming surf competition, but he never forgets about me. We haven't completely hashed out our Rah issue, but I honestly think we're both too busy to deal with unnecessary bull. We're here for each other and that's the most important thing. I can feel Jeremy's breath slow down as he falls back asleep, and I'm going to attempt to join him for the little time we've got left before our school day officially begins.

Jeremy and I got in a couple of good hours of sleep the second time around, but it wasn't enough to shake off my bad dream. I've been paranoid all morning and it's only our nutrition break. My girls haven't noticed my edgy mood, but I feel anything but cool. Laura and Reid making their way down the hall toward my locker can't be a positive thing. Unless they're coming to apologize for yesterday's hating in drama class, I don't want to hear it.

"Good morning, Jayd," Reid says. Laura's silent, allowing her man to do the talking this morning. "Laura and I want to apologize for upsetting you yesterday, especially knowing that you're trying out for the cheer squad. We might have to work with each other next year, and we don't want to start off on the wrong foot." Is this dude serious?

"Unless you've changed legs recently, you'll always be on the wrong foot with me," I say, shutting my locker door and facing them fully. "What do you really want, Reid? I'm not in the mood for your not-so-witty conversation today," I say, impressing Reid with a little wit of my own.

"Look, Jayd. Here's the deal," Reid says, clearing his throat. "We're going into our senior year, and the competition for solid activities for our college application is only going to get tougher. It's simply unfair that you'll probably get special consideration for everything because of your heritage, and we need you to let someone else have a shot at the good stuff, the lead role in the spring play included." I get it now. Laura needs to fill up her high school resume like I do, and she surely can't try out for cheer with her frail ass. She's already in ASB, and everything else is probably uninteresting to the little princess. No wonder the newfound curiosity with drama.

"Good-bye, Reid," I say, walking past him and toward my second period English class. I've still got a few minutes left before the bell rings and I'd rather spend them alone than with this racist fool and his girlfriend. Little does he know I get no special love because I'm the only black girl on the Advanced Placement track, and I wouldn't give up a damn thing even if I did.

"Jayd, I'm serious," Reid says, touching my shoulder like Esmeralda did in my dream this morning. "Just think about it. You wouldn't want to get hurt taking on too much." Reid and Laura smile, knowing they've shaken me to my core, but how? Misty's up to her evil tricks again. I know it. Before I can probe their minds, they walk off, leaving me in the main hall completely confused.

"Jayd, you look shook up this morning. Everything all right?" Mr. Adewale asks, being his usual observant self as he walks past me on the way to his classroom, which is also in the language hall adjacent to the main hall. I hope he didn't witness Reid and Laura talking to me, but I already know his hazel eyes don't miss a thing. I bet Nellie wishes her fake eyes gave her a little extra insight when it comes to her boyfriend, because he's changing right in front of us all and I think she's missing the signals.

"Bad dream," I say, not wanting to get into the details of my morning. Mr. Adewale shares my lineage and gifts because his family and Mama both lived in the same African village in South Carolina for a while, so I don't need to explain myself to him. He gets it, but I still don't want to talk about it. I follow him to his classroom and plop down in one of the seats.

"Ah," he says, propping himself up on the corner of his well-organized but packed desk. "Want to talk about it?" I look into his eyes, noticing the flecks of green circling the golden brown irises that make him that much more attractive to me. I look up at his bushy brown eyebrows and then to the crown of locks cascading loosely over his shoulders. This man is gorgeous and I know he feels me feeling him. I snap back into reality, feeling a bit warmer than usual.

"Not really." I look down at my worn sandals, realizing I need to hit up Payless shoes soon and stock up on my summer footwear. DSW has good sales, too, and they're both at the mall. Maybe Mickey will feel up to a shopping trip this week since Nellie's fallen off the deep end of the frenemies pool again. It's been a while since we hung out at the mall, and she could use the walking. Mr. A tosses his keys onto his desk, revealing yet another piece of his personal puzzle.

"You're in a fraternity?" I ask, shocked that Mr. Adewale would ever pledge anything. He seems like a "me phi me" kind of guy, but the black and red logo on the brass key chain is definitely from one of the black fraternities.

"Yes, and I'm a Mason. What of it?" He looks down at his keys and back at me, smiling at my reaction. I can never figure this brother out.

"I just never pegged you for a follower," I say, looking at the students walking by the open door, enjoying the warm weather. I would be out there, too, if my crew weren't dispersed all over the place. Nigel, Jeremy, and Chance are in the lower parking lot checking out Chance's latest car radio addition, and my girls are in the bathroom primping away the few minutes we have left in the morning break.

"You should never make assumptions about what you don't know, Jayd. Fraternities and sororities do a lot of good and serve their purpose, just like everything else in life. You can ask your grandmother about it, too."

"Yeah, I just found out she pledged in college, but I haven't talked to her about it yet." That's because I'm still in shock. There is so much about Mama I don't know, and the more I find out, the more I feel like I don't know my grandmother at all.

"She's also an Eastern Star, even though I know she hasn't been active since leaving the church."

"Are you serious?" I ask, ever shocked at the fact that Mr. A knows so much about my lineage. It's good insight but still a bit scary. "How come I never knew about that, either?" I know I said that aloud, but I'm really asking myself. How could I be so oblivious?

"Maybe you should ask more about your lineage and worry less about your little friends and their distractions," he says, gesturing toward the door. I guess he did witness the verbal combat I just experienced. "There's always more to learn, especially with the Williams women, no?" Mr. A is right. I've been off my spiritual game lately and I'm paying the price. I feel like honing my and my mom's talents is more important than my spiritual studies right now, but obviously I need to balance them both out.

Acknowledging my silence, Mr. A continues. "It's just a suggestion, Miss Jackson. I know you're a teenager and want to be like everyone else, but it's impossible, Jayd, because you're not a part of the status quo and never will be."

"Thanks for the pep talk, Mr. Adewale," I say, rising from my seat with the ringing bell. I could stay here and chat with Mr. A forever.

"Anytime, Jayd. See you in class next period," he says as I leave the room. I have a lot of work to catch up on and will check out more about Mama's path when I get a chance—sororities, secret societies, and all. Unfortunately it won't be this afternoon because I have to go to work after cheer practice. Yesterday was the introduction to what we're expected to learn by Friday, and the three routines are anything but easy. I'm sure this afternoon will be no different. At least today's the mandatory faculty meeting, allowing us all an early afternoon and me more time to spend with Mama and Netta. It'll be nice being around people who have my back after having to watch it all day at school.

The rest of the afternoon was pretty uneventful. Because my group already read through our parts for drama, the rest of the students had a free period to study our lines for the final round of auditions. Chance was conveniently missing in action. He can't avoid talking about his trip forever. If I didn't have cheer now, I'd go over to his house and get the full story. I've been rehearsing my dance moves since sixth period and am ready for today's rehearsal.

Stepping into the gym from the weight room where my class is held, I notice Nellie and Misty already dressed out. Please tell me Misty's not joining the tryouts. Oh hell no. We can't be in the same place at the same time for any longer than necessary. As if I didn't already have enough negative energy around, my nemesis has thrown her hat into the ring.

"What's up, Nellie?" I ask, trying to make nice, but I can see from Nellie's hazel glare that she's not done tripping off of Mrs. Carmichael's dinner invitation. If Nellie only knew the whole story maybe she wouldn't be so quick to hate on a sistah. But it's Chance's story to tell, not mine, and why he can't share it with his girlfriend is none of my business, either.

"Is she the only person standing here?" Misty asks, talking out of the side of her neck as usual. Rather than answer the evil wench, I choose to ignore her like Nellie did me, and claim a space on the half-court mark for practice. Before I can pass them both up, Misty sticks her fat foot out, tripping me on purpose.

"Ouch!" I exclaim, falling to the hard floor. "You bitch," I say, attempting to jump to my feet, but my skinned knee stops me from choking Misty, who's visibly pleased with her work. She's going to pay for this.

"Jayd, are you okay?" Nellie asks, feigning interest. I know she wants to laugh, but wants to keep from getting pimp slapped by me more.

"I'm fine," I say, glaring at Misty as I limp back toward the girl's locker room where Alicia, Shauna, and the rest of the cheer squad are busy prepping. The entire purpose of trying out is to better my chances at getting into college. Fighting with Misty won't help my ultimate goal. Maybe that's why Misty's really here: to test me. If that's the case, I sure as hell can't let her win.

"Jayd, you're bleeding," Alicia says, rushing toward me. "How'd you do that?" Alicia helps me to a bench and signals for Shauna to get the first aid kit.

"A big, fat foot came out of nowhere and tripped me, but I'm okay." I take the Band-Aid and alcohol pad from Shauna and clean myself up, trying to keep a cool head.

"I've noticed you've got some girls jealous of you already," Shauna says, looking out of the locker room toward Misty and Nellie. "It's all a part of it, Jayd. But don't worry, you'll fix them good at tryouts next week." Shauna's right. I'll shut them both up once I get the routines down. Until then, I'll just have to deal with the backstabbing heffas and get my job done—skinned knees, bad dreams, and all.

After a grueling cheer practice, I made my way to Compton, ready to work and forget about Nellie, Misty, and Laura, but there's no chance of that happening. Wearing my dance shorts inside the beauty shop where Mama and Netta could see the big patch covering my knee was my first mistake.

Telling Mama about my day—starting with my crazy dream right down to Misty making me fall—was the second.

Mama used the opportunity to say "I told you so" to her advantage, in more ways than one. She and Netta got to nurse my knee back to near-perfect health, scold me for not wearing my bracelets again, and give me another assignment to be completed immediately. I have to make a potion to protect me against my enemies, which isn't a bad thing. With the girls at South Bay High—also known as Drama High, and for good reason—I need all the help I can get. I also have to pray five times a day and always wear my jade bracelets until further notice. It's been a long day, making me grateful for the setting sun causing orange and red hues to scatter along the yellow wall in the small kitchen. I love being in the backhouse in the evening. Jeremy's not coming over to my mom's place until later tonight, giving me time to take a much-needed nap after I finish my spirit work.

Mama's trust in my driving skills has grown, but she'd still rather walk home from the beauty shop than ride as my regular passenger. She said to meet her here so she can check my work and provide the final blessing, but that was over an hour ago and a sistah's hungry. There's nothing back here to eat so I'll have to raid the house kitchen.

I step over a sleeping Lexi at the threshold and close the door behind me. Walking through the backyard I notice Misty across the way in Esmeralda's kitchen, probably doing something very similar to what I'm doing. It's strange how Misty and I can be so much alike at home but sworn enemies at school.

"Where'd you come from?" Bryan asks as I open the back door, stepping into the kitchen. It looks like he just got home from working at Miracle Market up the street. I'm just in time to mooch some dinner off my favorite uncle.

"I was in the back working on my mind. I need to get focused," I say, not boring Bryan with details he's not interested in. Mama gave me an early afternoon to get some work done and I appreciate the rare gift. It seems like the next test she and Netta are giving me is a big one. The subject matter is all about self-control and self-preservation, both of which are essential components of true progress of any kind. And I need to sharpen my saw in more ways than one.

"What, you think you're a Jedi warrior or some shit now?" Bryan asks, pretending the spatula is a lifesaver. He's making his specialty: home fries and a turkey burger. Maybe if I ask really sweet he'll hook his favorite niece up with some dinner.

"Yeah, I guess so, and that makes you Yoda, except you're not that wise; just old, short, and shriveled," I say, snatching the wooden spatula from Bryan and tossing it in the sink. Even he has to laugh at that one. I miss being in the kitchen with my favorite uncle. I even miss my cousin, Jay, who's busy bringing in the rest of the groceries. Daddy must've had a busy morning to do the grocery shopping in the afternoon. He's usually up and out right after I leave for school, knocking out his main daily chore before he's gone for the day. What a preacher does at church every day, all day, is still a mystery to me, but that's my grandfather's life and his business.

"Can I be Darth Vader?" Jay asks, coming in all late on the conversation and placing the plastic bags on the kitchen table. We all used to have a ball role-playing back in the day. I wish life were still that simple.

"Not if I have anything to say about it," Bryan says, reclaiming the spatula and smacking Jay on the head. Jay picks up a kitchen towel and returns the hit while I look through the bags for something to snack on. There's got to be some Ritz crackers in here or something.

"Hey, Tweet," Daddy says, bringing in the last of the groceries before heading back to church. I take the two bags from my grandfather and place them with the others.

"Hey, Daddy," I say, kissing him on the cheek and continuing my hunt. He looks at me feverishly searching through the bags and laughs. I don't see what's funny. I'm serious about my hunger.

"Here's some gas money or you can use it for food, little birdie," he says, kissing the top of my head and passing me twenty dollars.

"Thank you, Daddy. It'll go to good use," I say, folding the bill and tucking it securely in my jean pocket. That will fill up my tank for the rest of the week. He's such a good grandpa. I just wish he were a better husband to Mama, but that's not my business, either.

"You're welcome, baby. And tell your Mama and Karl I said hi," Daddy says, stepping out of the back door. "Bryan and Jay, get in here and put up these groceries. Jayd don't live here, but you two do and have to earn your keep, you hear?" Daddy yells at my cousin and uncle, who are now in the living room wrestling. Daddy winks at me before closing the door. We both know that even if I don't sleep here every night, this will always be my home. I turn off the stove, noticing my uncle's fries are done. Even with the kitchen in its naturally disheveled state, I miss cooking with my folks. I take the strainer out of the cluttered dish rack, line it with paper towels and reclaim the spatula for its proper use.

"Give up, boy, before you get hurt," Bryan says to Jay, pinned on the living room floor. They're like lion cubs in the jungle, I swear. While removing the fried potatoes from the skillet and placing them in the strainer to drain, I can't help but snack on a few. They taste as good as they smell and are perfectly seasoned, as always.

Mama made sure the youngest of us were in the kitchen

learning from the boss herself. The eldest of her children don't have the same knack for throwing down on the regular because Mama was too busy in the church and apparently pledging sororities and whatnot when she was younger. I can't wait to grill her about her school days when she finally gets home.

"Thanks," Bryan says, rescuing his fries before I can eat them all. "By the way, I ran into Rah the other day. He says to tell you hi." My uncle leans up against the kitchen counter, devouring his dinner and making me jealous.

"Who cares?" I ask, resuming my search for food. I luck up on a box of graham crackers and dig in. These should hold me until dinner.

"I care," Bryan says, damn near finished already. "It's causing him to be off his basketball game and that means money for the team. This shit has got the boy off his hustle, Jayd, and that's not good for anyone. This is street ball, not school yard playing."

"You make it sound like it's my fault," I say, walking in front of him to the refrigerator. I need some milk to make this meal complete, and less unwarranted guilt from my uncle to make it more pleasant.

"He's trying to be a good daddy, Jayd. Cut him some slack and be easy." I take a cup from the cupboard and pour my milk, ignoring my relentless uncle. Him and Rah go back to when Rah started balling in elementary school, hanging with the big boys from jump. Bryan has always taken a liking to him and therefore always in my ear defending him when he gets the chance. "You're only in high school. Stop taking shit so seriously all the time." Before I can question his ill logic, there's a knock at the front door. Jay rises from the couch and answers.

"Alaafia. Is Iya Lynn Mae available?" I hear someone ask Jay through the front door in a traditional greeting for people in our religious culture. Mama's clients usually know better than to drop by unannounced. Maybe he's new.

"Jayd," Jay calls, knowing I'll know what to do. I leave my uncle in the kitchen and walk through the dining room toward the front door. When I reach the screen I see a familiar face staring back at me from the porch: Emilio, with an elder I don't recognize.

"Jayd," Emilio says, as surprised as I am. I open the wrought-iron screen door and step onto the porch, closing it behind me. How did he know where we live?

"Yes, may I help you?" I ask, thrown off a little by the unexpected visit. I already have enough mixing of school and home drama with Misty occasionally staying next door with her evil godmother, Esmeralda. I don't need this fool hanging around, too.

"I didn't know that you were related to the iyalosha," Emilio says, referring to Mama by her spiritual title. Indeed, she is a mother with the orisha, but she's also a queen and he probably doesn't recognize her crown because she's African American. Emilio and I have already had it out about blacks in America and our role in the retention of traditional African religion versus South Americans and Cubans, who he is convinced saved our ancestors from extinction while we let them go. My blood boils just thinking about his smug words.

"Lynn Mae is my grandmother and she's also not here. Can I help you with something?" I repeat, anxious to get him off the porch.

"Emilio, is this the same Jayd you attend school with?" the elder asks, looking at me in amazement, apparently seeing the irony in our chance meeting, too.

"*Si, Papi. La misma,*" he says. Hell yeah, I'm the same Jayd, and I can see he's been running his mouth about me. But I really can't say shit because Mama and Netta know all about Emilio, too.

"So you're the new princess," the elder says, bowing his head in respect. Emilio looks on in awe of the man's reverence, but shows me the same respect. I return the greeting, waiting for the reason why they're dropping by unannounced. We just don't do that around here, and when Mama finds out I'm sure she'll put them in check.

"Please forgive my rudeness. *Me llamo* Baba Hector and you already know my godson, Emilio. We are seeking your *abuela*'s assistance with a most urgent matter," Hector says, almost pleading. Just their luck, Mama's walking up the block from Netta's shop now. Good. I want her to meet the infamous Emilio I told her about.

"My grandmother sees people by appointment only, but you can talk to her yourself," I say, pointing behind them. The elder turns around, relieved at the sight of Mama close to home.

"Jayd, I did not realize that you were related to the Queen Jayd," Emilio says, almost whispering he's so embarrassed by his ignorance. "This changes everything." I look at this fool, ready to go off, but Mama's here and I have to keep my composure in front of the elders.

"Greetings," Mama says, walking up the driveway toward the front porch. Lexi comes across the front lawn to greet Mama and check out the company, just in case her protection is needed. "Can I help you?" Mama steps up the three steps onto the porch with Lexi at her side. The dog looks at our company and is on guard, as she should be and should've been when they first arrived, but Lexi only works for Mama.

"Beni, iyalosha. I sincerely hope so," Hector says, bowing to Mama's invisible crown. Emilio follows suit and Mama touches both of their shoulders three times, indicating that they may rise. This shit is always so deep to me. It still throws me a little because Mama is my grandmother and I know her to be a great cook and the woman who can beat my ass if necessary. All of the reverence people pay her and me because of the women in our lineage just comes with the territory.

"How so?" Mama hands me her purse, keeping her workbag tightly tucked under her right arm. Her salt-and-pepper hair is loosely curled around her shoulders, framing her flawless face perfectly. Mama looks great for a sistah in her fifties and a mother of eight children. Her green eyes begin to glow as her irritation at the drop-by visit becomes more evident.

"I apologize for the intrusion, but we did not know how else to reach you. *Me llamo* Hector and this is my godson, Emilio," he repeats for Mama's sake, since I haven't had a chance to introduce them properly. Mama looks at me, recognizing my classmate's name, and I nod my head in acknowledgment that he is indeed the same Emilio I told her about some time ago. She turns her attention back to our guest, as curious as I am about the real reason they're here and who really sent them.

"Alaafia, Hector, Emilio. I am a busy woman, as I'm sure you can understand," Mama says, getting straight to the point. And I need to get going sooner than later if I'm going to get any studying done. Cheer tryouts were brutal today and it was only day two, so a hot bath is in order and so is a hot meal. I'm not sure if Mama has something else for me to do, which is why I'm waiting around. Otherwise I would've been out of here an hour ago.

"*Sí*, iyalosha. The reason for our visit is simple," Hector says, shifting from his left leg to the right, which is supported by a walking stick. He's a handsome man, his hair color matching Mama's. He's a bit on the short side, but that makes him even cuter in my eyes. I wonder how Emilio managed to hook up with a spiritual family in California when he's an exchange student from Venezuela. Maybe Mr. Adewale introduced them, since Emilio is his protégé now. Or maybe Emilio has some family here. Either way, it's a small world—too small, if you ask me.

"We need a new godmother in our ile," Emilio says, interrupting the elder, who shoots Emilio a look that says it all. Emilio bows his head in shame but still smiles at the cat finally being out of the bag.

"*Sí,* Emilio is correct. We need a new iyalosha for our spiritual house and you, of course, are the greatest there is, Queen Jayd. Would you consider it, *por favor?*" Hector's smooth, but no one's that good. Mama has always said it would be a cold day in hell before she went back to an ile or a church, and I'm pretty sure hell is still on fire. Being solely devoted to a spiritual house outside of our own is too much like church for Mama's blood.

"*Gracias,* señor, for your consideration, but I work for myself. But please feel free to call when you need assistance. I help the community whenever I can," Mama says, passing them both up and heading for the front door. I open the iron screen for her, but Hector didn't get the message. Lexi places herself between Mama and our guest, ready to get rough if necessary.

"Iya, *por favor,*" Hector pleads, grabbing Mama's right hand. She looks at him like he's lost his mind. I see touching folks out of the blue runs in their spiritual lineage. Emilio kissed me without my permission and then accused me of leading him on when I wasn't receptive to his arrogant ass. Hector doesn't look like he deals with rejection well, either. I look through the dining room and into the kitchen where the rest of Bryan's food is on the table. He and Jay are completely oblivious to the drama going on out here and I'd much rather be inside eating with them than dealing with this bull any day.

"Please let go of my hand," Mama says in a deep voice that immediately lets Hector know he's gone too far. "And like I already told you, I work alone. Now please leave. I have work to do." Hector reluctantly lets go of Mama's hand and she goes in the house, leaving Lexi to walk them off of the front porch. They can argue if they want to, but Lexi doesn't ask twice as her growl indicates. Both men look down at our healthy German shepherd and back up at me with pleading eyes, but I'm much less sympathetic than they think.

"Princess Jayd, talk to your *abuela, por favor,*" Hector says. "We are in desperate need of her powerful female energy. My wife has taken ill and I can't manage our house alone." Lexi walks slowly toward them, urging them off the porch. I swear Lexi is more human than we give her credit for. One step at a time the men walk down while continuing to beg.

"I feel for your loss, Baba Hector, but my grandmother can't be swayed. Odabo," I say. They both return the traditional good-bye and finally leave. I know Emilio will be all up in my ear at school from now on, like he needs another reason to talk to me. I'd better check on Mama in the spirit room. I bypass my uncle and cousin, making my way through the kitchen and back outside.

"Someone's always trying to put me on spiritual lockdown, I swear," Mama says, furiously washing her hands in the kitchen sink. Her workbag is on the table and I place her heavy purse next to it. Mama takes one of the two yellow towels hanging from the refrigerator door to dry her hands.

"It's not such a bad thing to be asked, is it? It's like a compliment to your flyyness," I say, trying to make her smile, but Mama's too pissed to see the humor in the situation.

"Jayd, please. They didn't come all the way over here to stroke my ego for my own good. Trust me, the benefit would be all theirs." Mama opens the large hemp bag, removing its contents and putting everything in its place. She and Netta were busy mixing various concoctions of creams, oils, and bath salts when I arrived at work this afternoon and they were having a good time doing it. Sometimes I think they miss having the shop all to themselves, before my young self invaded their serene space. I'm just glad they let a sistah share in the wealth.

"What's so wrong about them wanting you to be their spiritual house mother, especially if it's because a family member fell ill?" I wash my hands, realizing I won't be leaving as soon as I'd hoped.

"People go to war all the time, just like in real families. And I guarantee they think their original iyalosha fell ill because of some spiritual backlash, and now they're looking to replace her and gain revenge against the other house. Trust me, Jayd. This is no innocent inquiry. I felt his desperation before he touched me," she says, changing out of her street clothes and into her whites. "Now I have to do a cleansing on myself to get rid of that negative-energy dumbass," she says, wrapping her freshly done head in a white cloth before getting to work.

"So how do you know when to help someone and when not to?" I ask, following her lead. I claim the basic staple ingredients for a head cleansing from the various glass jars lining the counter: coconut, cocoa butter, and white chalk. Mama will handle the rest. My job is always the grating, and these three items have to be grated to perfection. I might as well get to work.

"When it's all about the religion and not the individuals in it. If it doesn't feel good—or God, as I like to say—don't do it." Mama used to tell me that all the time and I must say, she's right. "So much about religion—be it social, personal, cultural—is about repression, sacrifice, and hatred. Separating 'us' from 'them' and then feeling self-righteous about the shit is the creed; doubt and fear are the practice. That sounds too much like prison to me." Mama's on point with that observation.

I'm not down for any type of incarceration, spiritual or otherwise, and neither are the women in my lineage. We may be bound by blood, but our associations are our own. I'm so thankful for female wisdom, and it couldn't have come at a better time. With Misty, Laura, and Nellie working overtime to secure my demise, I'm liable to slip up and keep myself from getting into a good school. I've got to learn to keep my cool completely when they get on my nerves.

You sure do, baby, because schoolgirls never go away, ever, my mom says, adding her two cents to our mother-granddaughter moment. Mama looks at me, feeling the presence of her elder daughter in the room and smiles. *So listen to Mama and do everything she tells you to keep the haters at bay. 'Bye,* my mom says, exiting my thoughts as quickly as she appeared.

"Your mother's right, Jayd," Mama says, already tapped into our telepathic conversation. "Listen to me and do everything I say, starting with helping me strengthen this potion of yours after our head cleansings. Then you can go home and get some rest." All of the above sounds good to me, especially the part about me getting some sleep. Mama looks like she could use some, too. It's been a long day for us both and tomorrow will most likely be the same drama, just a different day.

~ 6 ~
School Daze

*"Now I got my foot through the door/
And I ain't going nowhere."*

—EVE FEATURING GWEN STEFANI

The morning fog is thick, limiting my visibility on the way from Inglewood to Compton, but luckily I can drive this route with my eyes closed. After Mama and I finished our work last night, I left my prescribed potion on the shrine to be blessed by the ancestors. I had to leave for school twenty minutes earlier than I normally would to make the necessary detour to pick up the potion. With the ASU officer elections today and cheer tryouts on Friday, I'm going to need all the help I can get against Misty and my other school haters to make it through the next three days.

I park the car in front of my grandparents' house and quickly make my way to the backhouse. Locating the small green vial on the shrine, I say a short prayer and walk out of the spirit room and through the backyard without disturbing anyone sleeping in the main house. Locking the gate behind me, I look back, thinking I heard something, but I'm alone, or so I think. With my car parked on the street, I've left myself open to an unwelcome morning visitor.

"You're looking more and more like your mother every day," Esmeralda says to me from the safety of her enclosed front porch. I'm sure she's noticed I've moved out and that means Misty knows my family business, too. I know better than to look the wench in her evil blue eyes, but she's making it difficult to avoid her icy glare. There's something about Esmeralda that pulls you to look at her, almost like a magnet for eyes. As many times as I've been crippled by Esmeralda's vision in one way or another, I've learned my lesson.

"I'll take that as a compliment," I say. Keeping my eyes to the ground, I quickly walk toward my mom's car, stepping out into the street and walking around to the driver's side rather than remaining on the sidewalk, trying to keep as much distance between us as possible. I open the driver's side door and place the bag of goodies inside. Along with my potion I also grabbed some more belly balm for Mickey. I hope she appreciates it.

"You should. Your mother was a worthy adversary, just like you and your grandmother," Esmeralda says, coming to the front of her gated porch and holding the bars like she's in prison. I guess living in that pet infested, worn-down home is like a cell, especially with the warden living next door. She's being hella bold this morning, speaking to me when she knows Mama will have her ass if she finds out.

"Lynn Marie's a beautiful girl. I remember the day she was born. You do know I was her godmother at one time and that I helped to deliver her, don't you?" No longer able to resist her magnetic glare, I stare into Esmeralda's eyes, unwillingly sharing her memory. The vision of Mama in labor with her firstborn snaps to the front of my mind like a movie. I can see Mama pushing and Esmeralda there to catch my mother.

"That was a long time ago," I say, shaking the vision out of my head. How did she do that? I don't want to see anything this woman has to offer, nor did I intend to get inside her head. I force my eyes back down, breaking my vision quest with Esmeralda.

"When your mother lost her sight it was a terrible loss for

us all." What did she just say to me? I knew she and Misty gave me the head cold I mysteriously caught on my birthday, which was a direct result of me attempting to tap into Misty's convoluted mind. But using my mom's vision against me is a whole other thing completely.

"Since you caused the loss, I doubt you're that sorry about it. And you're not a part of my family or our lineage, no matter what role you once played," I say, trying to get in the car. I again try to keep from looking up, but my head is hot and her eyes are cool, pulling me toward her.

"All is not completely lost, is it, little Jayd?" Esmeralda asks, her eyes becoming too cool for me to handle. I don't feel so good.

"Can we help you, Esmeralda?" Mama asks, stepping onto the front porch and freeing me from the conversation. Esmeralda always sends chills up my spine, usually resulting in me having a headache or worse. I don't have time to be sick today.

"Not yet, but I'll let you know soon," Esmeralda says before retreating back into her house. What was that all about? Mama walks down the porch steps and I walk toward her, meeting halfway up the driveway where Daddy's Cadillac is parked. She checks me out with her eyes, causing me to feel better already. Mama looks as worried about Esmeralda's last response as I am.

"We'll talk about it later, Jayd," Mama says, feeling me. "Never engage that old crow again, you hear me?" I wish it were that easy. And now that same crow knows I've regained possession of my mom's gift of sight. That can't be good, especially since I haven't even told Mama yet.

"I tried to ignore her, Mama, but she has some sort of pull." Mama looks at my left arm, noticing I forgot to wear my bracelets again and I can't say shit. But at least this time they're in the car.

"Wear your bangles at all times, Jayd. What good is having protection if you don't use it?" She's got a point there.

"Okay, Mama. I will. They're in my purse—I just forgot to put them on once I got in the car this morning," I explain on my way back to my mom's Mazda. "I'm even wearing a green vest to match for good luck," I say, waving to Mama. I have to get going if I want to make it to school in Redondo Beach on time.

"I love you, baby, and remember to use what you've got," Mama says, reminding me to not only sport my bangles but also to use my potion. I have a busy day ahead of me and with the way my morning started, it's going to be an interesting school day, to say the least. All that matters in the end is if it turns out my way, starting with me being referred to as ASU president.

The rest of my day has been pretty full so far, yet all I can think about is my run-in with Esmeralda this morning. I don't know what Misty and her wicked godmother are up to now, but it's got me nervous as all get-out. If Esmeralda tries to use my mother's powers for her own benefit and Mama finds out I kept it from her, that's my ass no matter how it goes. My jade bracelets are in place and the potion has been taken, making me as ready as I'll ever be for the vote in a few minutes.

I was supposed to meet Chance as soon as the lunch bell rang five minutes ago, but he's not here yet. We not only have to be on time for the meeting in order to vote, but we also need to find time to rehearse for our auditions next period, and he hasn't even memorized his lines yet. What the hell is up with my boy? Maybe I should take up his mom on her dinner invitation and have a little talk with her, ganging up on my friend all the while. As long as Mr. Carmichael's not there I can take it. A free dinner's a free dinner, no matter whose house it's served at.

"What's crackin'?" Chance asks, walking into the quad outside of our speech class, looking like he's straight out of a Ludacris video. What the hell?

"Hey, Chance. I see you went on a little shopping spree while in the A last weekend, huh?" I'm used to him dressing like the hip-hop head he is, but the sparkly jeans hanging off his ass and matching gaudy belt is a bit much for me. And if it's too much for me, I know it's going to be over-the-top for his preppy girlfriend.

"Scratch that Chance shit, baby. My name is Chase, like the bank, because I'm paid, you feel me?" Chance says, smiling and showing off his new gold grill. He did not come back from a weekend down South with some gold and diamonds covering his teeth. This can't be real. Nellie, Mickey, and Nigel join us just in time for the one-man fashion show. I wonder if Nellie has seen this new Chance today. He was absent from fourth period but here now for all to see.

"Hey, baby," Nellie says, ignoring me, but she can't ignore her man. Astronauts in space can see Chance's bright attire and accessories from where he's standing.

"What's up with you, shawty?" Chance asks Nellie, attempting to kiss her, but she's too blinded by his smile for that.

"What the hell is that in your mouth?" Nellie screams, reaching up and grabbing her man by the jaw. I guess she's just as surprised as I am by our friend's transformation. Chance gladly parts his lips, allowing the world to see his new bling. Nigel and Mickey look impressed at the jewelry and Nellie looks equally disgusted.

"Damn, look at all that ice. Your grill's worth more than my ride," KJ says admiringly as he passes us by to enter our classroom, ready to vote for himself for president, I assume. Del and Money are right along with him, eyeing Chance's new mouth gear like kids in a candy store. I know they're secretly hating on Chance's money. They can only dream of having a grill worth a quarter of what that one costs.

"Yeah, man. It probably is. I got it made when I was down South. I had to have it set right when I got back and now it fits like butter, baby. Know what I'm saying?" Chance says, putting his arm around Nellie's shoulders and attempting to kiss her again, but she's not having it. From what I know of my girl, Chance is becoming her worst nightmare overnight, and vice versa. The last thing Chance wants is a wannabe white girl, and Nellie will be damned if she dates anyone hood—rich and white or not.

"No, I don't know what you're saying nor do I want to as long as you're talking with that thing in your mouth," Nellie says, pushing Chance's face hard before storming into the classroom, and I'm right behind her. I've had enough of the new Chase for one day. Ever since he got back from Atlanta he's been a different person: name, teeth, and all. I miss my old friend. I should've kept my mouth shut about him having some black in him and he probably would never have found out about being adopted. Well, at least not on my watch. I just hope Chance's new look hasn't completely clouded his judgment and he votes right.

"Let's get started, young people," Mr. Adewale says as the fifteen or so club members settle down. Ms. Toni walks in and takes her customary seat behind his desk as Mr. A continues from his post by the board. "I know we're all anxious to finally get this vote over with and our officers settled for next year," Mr. Adewale says, passing out the voting packets containing the anonymous speeches for each office.

"You'll have fifteen minutes to read each speech and then

vote for your favorite ones for each office. Any questions?"
Ms. Toni says, winking at me as she glances around the room.

"Yeah. Can we identify our speech after we vote?" KJ asks.
That's actually not a bad question.

"Yes, you can. Remember, you're voting silently; there's
absolutely no communication allowed. Read the words carefully and consider each speech separate from personalities."
Ms. Toni and Mr. Adewale serve as guards for the tensest fifteen minutes of my life. I, of course, know my own words.
But judging strictly off of someone else's written words is
more difficult than I thought it would be. What if one of
these letters belongs to Misty, and I accidentally vote her into
an office? That's just unacceptable to me, but I have to vote.

"Time," Mr. Adewale says. Here goes nothing. He collects
the papers and tallies the results with Ms. Toni. We're all too
nervous to chat it up so we eat our lunches in silence.

"Our new ASU officers are—" Ms. Toni says, adjusting her
glasses on the tip of her nose for dramatic effect. She loves
her job as the activities director and mentoring students and
teachers alike. "Our new secretary is Alia. The position of
treasurer will be held by Chance. Emilio is our vice president
and Jayd, you're our new president. Congratulations, everyone," Ms. Toni says, making my day. KJ, Misty, and the rest of
their crew look pissed off. I bet he doesn't want to identify
his speech now that he's lost.

"That's the bell, young people," Mr. Adewale says. "Our
next meeting will be the first you hold as officers. Let's make
it a good one," he says as Ms. Toni rises from her seat, giving
each of the officers a big hug.

"Jayd, I'm so proud of you," Ms. Toni says, whispering in
my ear. She can't show favoritism in front of the other students, but I can feel the love. "Now, please do me proud in
drama class, too."

"I'll do my best. See you later, Ms. Toni and Mr. Adewale,"
I say, walking with the rest of the crowd toward our fifth periods. Shae, Tony, Misty, and the rest of the South Central
crew look salty as hell. Oh well. They voted, too. It wasn't my
fault KJ's speech apparently sucked.

"Later, madam president," Mr. A says, no longer hiding his
enthusiasm for my victory. Madam president: I like the sound
of that. And I also like that we have a diverse cabinet for ASU.
Ever since hanging out with Alia, Charlotte, and the rest of
the AP study group last month, I like Alia's swag and think
she'll be a great asset. Emilio, on the other hand, is too much
of an ass kisser for me. But he won fair and square, so I have
to work with him whether I like it or not.

"Congrats, Lady J," Chance says, putting his arm around
my neck as we wave 'bye to Nigel and Mickey, who also congratulate us on our wins. Nellie doesn't say a word to either
of us and leaves before we can say anything to her. I guess
she's had enough excitement for one day.

"Congratulations to you, too. So are we ready for another
victory?" I ask. The blank look on Chance's face tells me he's
completely forgotten about the auditions this afternoon.
Shit. He can't do me like this—not now.

"Ah, baby, I completely forgot about the auditions today.
But I got you on the last round," he says, walking toward the
parking lot next to the drama room instead of the class itself.

"Chance, you can't skip out on me. I need you," I say, realizing he's on another mission that has nothing to do with
the play. "What the hell am I going to do about the dialogue
scene?"

"Girl, you don't need me. Besides, I told you I got you
next time. You know Mrs. S can't say no to me," he says,
walking toward his car, which he starts with his key-chain re-
mote. "I've got to get my new rims locked properly before
someone jacks me, girl. You understand," Chance says. Hell

no, I don't understand and I'm sure Chance can tell from my silence that he's going to pay for this little stunt, big-time. The final bell for fifth period rings, signaling my looming fate. If I don't have a partner for the scene, I forfeit my audition for the lead role just like that. I have to find someone else to read with and fast.

The line for auditions is long, with partners practicing outside, including Laura and Reid, who look thrilled to see me alone. While Chance or Chase or whoever he is today continues to go through his identity crisis, I'm still without a leading man. What the hell am I going to do now? I walk through the crowd and into the drama room on the way to the theater, anxious to sign up.

"Congratulations on your win, Jayd," Emilio says from where he's standing near the main stage door. What the hell is he doing all the way down here?

"Yeah, you too," I say, passing him by to find the sign-up sheet in its usual spot on the podium. I take the clipboard and flip the pages until I find an empty slot. With all five periods combined, there are over one hundred and fifty drama students, not to mention the other fifty or so students not in the class who want to try out for the last play of the year. Emilio continues standing over my shoulder and I continue trying to ignore him. I sign my name in one of four available slots for the dialogue auditions, praying someone comes through for me by the end of the period. This dude has a lot of nerve talking to me after that little show he and his godfather put on at Mama's house yesterday afternoon. I've successfully avoided Emilio all day long, but he's caught me off guard in the last place I'd expect to see him.

"Jayd, I couldn't help but notice you have no one to read the scene with," Emilio says, following me off stage and out of the theater.

"You could've helped if you weren't peeping over my

shoulder." I glance back at Emilio, shooting him an evil look before heading out the back door. It's a warm day, and being outside is better than sitting in the dark, air-conditioned class any day. Realizing I've left my playbook on the podium, I turn around and rush to the stage to retrieve it before some-one else picks it up, with Emilio right on my heels. What does he want now?

"I can be your leading man, if you can convince your grandmother to help us," Emilio says, stepping onto the stage. Did he hear what I just said? My mom's powers have been working overtime trying to beat Misty and Esmeralda at their own games. But I can't deal with Emilio and his prob-lems right now. I'm still high from winning the election a few minutes ago and this fool's taking it away.

"Emilio, give it a rest," I say, claiming the booklet.

"We don't have the gift like your grandmother's line. Had I known which house you were from, I would not have . . . ," he says, ready to beg, but I'm cutting his shit short. I have less than forty minutes to find another partner and he's wast-ing my time.

"You would not have what, Emilio?" I ask, cutting him off before he can force his foot any further down his throat. "Not demeaned Africans in America by saying we let our ancestors die, including my lineage?"

"Exactly. No, what I mean to say is that you are different," Emilio says, now breathing shoe polish.

"Different? That sounds worse than when white folks say that shit to me." I turn around and stare at the backdrop of costumes, scene changes, and other students anxiously re-hearsing scenes for the auditions all over the theater. They probably think we're rehearsing, too. Without a partner to perform with, I'll have to forfeit and possibly set myself up for a part in the chorus or as an extra, since this is my last opportunity for a solid A. I'm not going out like that, but I can't perform with this jerk, either.

"Jayd, please. I knew there was something special about you from the moment I first laid eyes on you. You shine, my princess." Emilio bends over and touches the ground, bowing to my head like devotees do when they greet Mama. Oh, now this fool is really tripping, doing this at school where everyone can see. I think I liked it better when Emilio was mad at me and thought I came from a long line of promiscuous women.

"Okay, enough with all of that," I say, pulling him up by his shoulder straps. I don't want to rip his backpack, but if he doesn't get up soon, it's over. "What do you really want?"

"Your *abuelita* as our iyalosha. What will it take? We will do anything she asks of us if she'll agree to join our house." Mama's not keen on joining any organizations—religious, social, or otherwise.

"Didn't she already tell you no? It's the same answer in Spanish, too, so I know you understood her the first time." Mrs. Sinclair calls the next couple into the drama room to audition. I'm up next with no Chance. What am I going to do?

"Jayd, we are desperate. Please, convince her it's the right road to take. Otherwise, we will have to ask someone else and she may not be happy with the result."

"Are you threatening my grandmother?" I ask, ready to punch this punk in his scheming mouth. Emilio's not to be trusted—ever. I knew that from our first encounter months ago when he decided to kiss me at lunch, causing more tension between Jeremy and me than we already had at the time.

"It only sounds like that because you're listening with your ego and not your mind," he says. "Just like the auditions, Jayd. It's a means to an end, that's all."

"You are something else, you know that? If you knew anything about my lineage you'd back the hell off while you still can," I say, ready to make some threats of my own. "This conversation is over," I say, picking up my script and heading for the classroom. If Chance doesn't show up I'll just have to deal with the disappointment on my own.

"Jayd, I've been looking for you all over the place, girl," Nigel says, jogging down the aisle. "Chance called me to come rescue you." Nigel hugs me and shows me his script.

"What are you talking about?" I ask, completely confused. Nigel's not an actor last time I checked. Emilio, not taking the hint, stands his ground. Doesn't he know when a girl's not interested?

"Jayd, you're up," Matt says. He, Seth, and Alia run all the behind-the-scenes production issues, including helping with auditions. "Where's Chance?" he asks, noticing my buddy's missing. Emilio smiles cunningly like he knows he's got me trapped.

"Here he is," I say, taking Nigel's hand and walking toward the side door leading to the drama room. Matt shakes his head, laughing at my joke and walks back through the door with us behind him. I look back at Emilio, whose smile has turned into a frown. Oh well. He should know better than to try and corner a Williams woman. We always find another way.

"Now you know this ain't my thing," Nigel says, looking nervously through the wrinkled script. "Chance said all I have to do is read the highlighted parts and I'm good."

"Just be yourself and you'll do fine," I say, squeezing my friend's hand. "And aren't you missing class right now?"

"I told my math teacher I wanted to audition for the spring play. Me and that old white dude don't get along at all; he was actually happy to see me go," Nigel says, opening the door facing Mrs. Sinclair and her groupies. She's the ultimate judge and jury, but her fan club gets to throw their opinions in the mix, too. "Chance sounded really bad about leaving you hanging, and I couldn't let my girl fall." I'm glad to know one of my school friends feels that way. Leave it to the heffas I thought were my best friends and I'd be down for the count.

"Thank you, Nigel. I owe you one," I say, ready to get the show on the road and this day over. And what a day it has been. First Esmeralda forced her way into my thoughts this morning, then I won the ASU election, and now Nigel's my drama partner. This has been the most unpredictable and exhausting day ever. I can't wait for Friday to arrive so I can chillax for a day or two. With the final day for cheer tryouts Friday afternoon and Jeremy's surf competition on Saturday, I'm sure it'll be a good weekend to get in some much needed quality time for me and my baby. We've both had so much on our plates we've barely had time to break bread together. We'll make up for it this weekend: no bitches, broads, or tricks allowed.

~ 7 ~
Hamburger Helper

*"I know my past ain't one you can easily get past /
But that chapter is done"*

—JAY-Z

It's been a long week. Wednesday was the longest day, start-ing with Esmeralda's evil ass and ending with Nigel be-coming my leading man. Now Nellie and Mickey are hating on me harder than ever before. When Nigel came to my res-cue Wednesday afternoon, Mickey found out about it and went off, saying that Nigel doesn't have time to be in a play, but Mrs. Sinclair thought differently, offering Nigel and me the parts on the spot. I was so surprised I almost kissed Nigel on the cheek but held back, and so did he. At first Nigel wasn't going to accept it, but he's reconsidering the offer. And once Nellie found out that Chance put him up to it, it was a wrap.

Nellie accused me of trying to turn their boyfriends against them, which is purely insane. Nigel's not going any-where, and Nellie's doing a good job of turning her man off all by herself. Things between Nellie and me are only bound to get worse if I make the squad this afternoon. Nellie will probably lose her mind if she doesn't make the cut, but it's not my fault the girl has no rhythm. They'll post the new cheerleaders' names in the gym at lunch, which is where I'm headed. The new squad will rehearse after school with plenty of celebrating to follow.

There's a large crowd around the gym announcement

board, Misty and Nellie included. There are girls everywhere, some screaming and most crying. From the look of it, Nellie's been crying her eyes out already.

"You made it!" Shauna exclaims, jumping up and down with Alicia right by her side. They both hug me and I can't help but join in the excitement. I feel bad for Nellie, but if it were the other way around I doubt she'd share the love. Alicia and Shauna let me go to continue the celebratory congratulations. Now that that's over, I can spend the rest of my lunch with Jeremy. I can't wait to share the news.

"This is my dream, Jayd. Get your own life," Nellie says, now frantically crying, she's so upset at the results. It's not my fault. All black people can't dance and she proved that at the solo tryouts yesterday. Nellie's good at following orders, but originality isn't her strongest feature. We could've rehearsed together, but she was too busy stabbing me in the back with her new best friend, Misty, to see clearly. Misty doesn't even look like she cares about not making the squad, which leads me to believe it was never about that at all. I knew that trick didn't want to be a cheerleader, so what's she really up to?

"Jayd's specialty is stealing other people's desires, isn't it?" Misty says, and we both know she's one step away from getting her curly head bit off, bringing up my mother's powers. I can't wait to get this broad once and for all. Lucky for her, my jade bracelets are keeping me cool and with my protection potion running through my veins, I know Misty's no threat to me this afternoon.

"You knew this was all about me, Jayd. How could you?" Nellie continues, completely self-absorbed. I hate to be the one to tell her, but with or without my presence, she doesn't have what it takes to be on the squad. If she had professional choreographers helping her, she still wouldn't be able to find her rhythm.

"This is my life, Nellie. You need to get a grip," I say, attempting to leave the gym, but Nellie won't shut up.

"How are you going to be president of ASU, star in a play with my boyfriend, be a debutante, and then cheer on top of it all?" I admit it's a busy schedule, but nothing I can't handle. A girl's got to push hard if she wants to make it to the top.

"It's not all at the same time, and two of the things are temporary, not that I need to explain my schedule to you," I say, walking past her toward the open door. "But some of us can walk, chew bubble gum, and juggle at the same time—no offense." Nellie's so visibly pissed she could have a stroke right there on the basketball court.

Yes, but too much can lead to a meltdown, and you don't want to go there, trust me, my mom says, quickly intervening with some advice of her own. But now is not the time for counseling. I won fair and square. Nellie and Misty need to back up before it really goes down. This isn't *Gossip Girl,* and I'm not all talk. I will hit a bitch if she keeps testing me, cool head or not.

"See, she's already acting strange, proving she's not fit to be a cheerleader," Nellie says, convincing herself more and more with each passing moment that there's been a large error made or that she's dreaming. I know how that feels and trust me, this isn't a dream. "It's not fair!" Nellie shouts, strands of blond hair sticking to her tear-streaked cheeks.

"Nellie, grow up," I say, tired of the tantrum. "Why can't you be happy for me as your friend, and not hating like the jealous bitch you've become?" I ask, now really on a roll. It was one thing for her to be upset because she lost, but another thing altogether for Nellie to continue pissing on my parade. Sure, I wasn't really planning on becoming a cheerleader. But like all challenges, I'm in it to win it and that I did.

Nellie's not up for labor of any kind; she knows it, I know it, and God knows it. She just wanted to join the pep squad for the popularity and perks that come with it, especially now that her Homecoming reign is officially coming to an end.

"Who you calling a bitch?" Nellie asks, her neck rolling and blond tresses waving. If I didn't know better, I'd say that Nellie was ready to throw down, but she's too prissy to fight, unlike Mickey, who'll bite off her acrylics to throw down if necessary. Nellie's trim French manicure would get chipped and that just wouldn't work for Little Miss Princess.

"You. I'm calling you a bitch. Isn't that your favorite home-girl word these days?" I ask, reminding Nellie that it was she who started that train. She's been using the word so damn much I started to believe it myself. "And you know what? I think it's quite an appropriate title for you, especially this year. You've been nothing but mean and rude and selfish, not only to me but to your boyfriend, who in spite of his recent confused behavior is very sweet and loyal to your stuck-up ass. So get a grip and celebrate someone else's happiness for a change." Finally shutting Nellie up, I march past her toward the rest of the newly appointed cheer squad to congratulate them before I head out.

"Hey, Jayd. If you want we're going to rehearse a little and celebrate at my house after school," Alicia says. "Not that you need much. It looks like you've got the moves down, but you know how the saying goes."

"Practice makes perfect," Shauna offers, like I wouldn't have figured it out myself. But I understand she's excited, so I'll let my smart-ass comment go for now.

"I wish I could, but I have to work this afternoon. Next time I'm there," I say. Noticing our little powwow, Nellie walks over, looking completely annoyed that the cheerleaders are paying me any mind. I guess she thought that as a member of ASB they would take a natural liking to her, but she was wrong.

"You could never be a cheerleader," Nellie says, her hazel eyes glowing with rage. Who the hell does she think she's talking to? Has this girl completely lost her mind or what? I look at Misty behind her, recognizing that iced-over glare anywhere: Esmeralda's running this show via Misty. And Nellie's hot head is the perfect receptor.

"Nellie, you need to slow your roll before these pom-poms aren't the only things getting tossed in the air." I want to help my girl, but she's making it very difficult for me to maintain my cool. Why is she so damn weak? If it weren't for her petty hating, Misty would've never been able to get in her mind in the first place.

"You see what I mean? She's too damn ghetto to represent this school. Can't you see that?" Shauna, Alicia, and the rest of the pep squad look on, dazed by the outburst.

"All I see is a hater on deck. Anybody else feel me?" I ask, making the cheerleaders and other spectators laugh at Nellie's irrational behavior. There must be over two hundred people in this gymnasium and every one of them just heard me. The warning bell for fifth period rings, breaking up our heated debate before it goes too far.

"This isn't over, Jayd," Nellie says, finally leaving and allowing me a brief moment of relief before heading to find Jeremy before fifth period begins. I know it's not over. With Misty's evil ass in the mix, it never is. But I won this round of school war all week long. I'm ready to give it a rest and get my hustle on.

Today's a perfect day to chill by the beach with what's left of my crew. Jeremy's competition is at the pier by the school, so I'm sure more school folks will be in attendance. Hopefully Laura and Reid will sit this gathering out. I've had enough of all of my haters for the week. Too bad the main ones also live in my hood.

Chance came to pick me up at my mom's apartment after I finished working this morning, to make up for ditching me at the auditions yesterday. He's also letting me drive his powerful classic hot rod, almost causing me to forgive him on the spot. It still hurts, but I understand he's going through a lot right now and school's probably the last thing on his mind. Nellie's not talking to him or me, putting us in the same boat. Nigel and Mickey are meeting us at the beach to support Jeremy. I doubt Mickey wanted to go, but after Nigel helped me out Wednesday, she's not letting him out of her sight.

"Damn, Jayd. Ease up on the pedal, baby. You're pushing it a little hard, ain't you?" Chance says, protective of the only baby he has, and for that, I am grateful. At least one of my male friends hasn't knocked somebody up. Technically Nigel didn't either, but he could've, and he's still the baby's daddy as far as we're all concerned.

"I'm like Rihanna up in here," I say, turning the stereo up louder and allowing Rihanna to sing my theme song as I fly down Pacific Coast Highway. We're arriving at the beach a little early to get a good seat. I'm going to take the opportunity to study my spirit work and relax in the sun. It's rare I get a Saturday afternoon to hang.

"You can pull up right here, Jayd," Chance says, pointing to an empty space not far from the shore. I park the car, turn off the engine and banging sounds, and hop out of the vehicle with my purse and backpack in tow.

"We should still be able to get a good seat," Chance says, pointing toward the water. There are people everywhere, including the competing surfers—my baby included. I catch Jeremy's eye and blow a kiss in his direction. He smiles at me and returns his attention to his surfboard. As we get closer to

where the competition's taking place, I see Nigel and Mickey
have already claimed a seat for us at one of the umbrella-
covered picnic tables, giving us an unobstructed view of the
ocean. I brought Mickey's belly balm that I meant to give her
on Wednesday, just in case she decides to play nice. I know
she must be itching for more by now.

"What's up, peeps?" Chance says, giving Nigel dap and
Mickey a hug. I put my things down on the table, hug Nigel,
and speak to Mickey as well.

"I'm going to grab a quick bite. Anyone else hungry?"
Chance asks.

"I'll take a pretzel," I say, reaching for my purse. Chance
gives me the same look Jeremy does when I try to pay.

"I know you didn't insult me like that, right?" Chance
asks. I put my purse back on the table and sit down across
from Mickey, who puts in her order, too.

"I'll come with you, man," Nigel says. "You're going to
need help carrying all the food." I grab my backpack, ready
to get my study on unless Mickey wants to apologize, which I
doubt.

Mickey and I sit in silence for a few moments after the
guys leave, neither one of us ready to take the first step toward reconciliation. I couldn't care less if she talks to me, but
it seems silly not to be friends right now. I should be overexcited about my recent triumphs and able to share them
with my girl, but instead I'm sitting here trying not to look
her in the eye. Mickey doesn't know it yet, but she's going to
need all the help she can get when that baby comes, and Nellie can't be counted on for something as serious as this.
Nickey will be born soon, and there's no time to make enemies out of old friends, especially not good ones.

I reach inside my bag and claim the small container of
belly balm to give to Mickey. Tired of the stank vibe, I decide
to be the bigger woman and suck it up.

"Truce?" I ask, sliding the yellow container across the table. Mickey looks at it and then up at me. Without saying a word, she takes the ointment, opens the top, lifts her stretched-out tank top and smears it all over her stomach, making us both laugh.

"Girl, I needed that," Mickey says, vigorously rubbing her skin. "I thought I was going to go crazy if I didn't get some more of this stuff. Thank you, Jayd." For Mickey, that's as close to an apology as I'm going to get, and I'll take it.

"You are very welcome," I say, reaching across the small table and feeling her hard stomach. It won't be long now.

"Look who's talking," Nigel says as he and Chance bring over the feast of junk food. Nigel looks more relieved that Mickey and I are cool than I do. I never thought how much stress it puts on Nigel when Mickey starts tripping on me. He was my friend first and will always be there for me, no matter how pissed off Mickey gets. I think she's starting to understand.

"Hey, there's Jeremy's team," Chance says, pointing at the surfers lining up at the water, ready to dive in. "They're starting now."

"Go Jeremy!" I yell at the top of my lungs. I doubt he heard me over the loud waves and other sounds from the busy crowd surrounding the shore this afternoon, but it was worth a shot.

"Kick some surfer ass, white boy!" Mickey yells, causing heads to turn. "What did I say?" Nigel, Chance, and I look at our girl and bust up laughing. This is just what we all needed. Hopefully it will stay this light all day and my baby will win the competition. That's all we need to make this day perfect.

After a few hours of surfing, the announcement is made. Jeremy's team came in first in two out of seven categories. I

still don't quite get it, but I'm glad, however it all adds up, that Jeremy came out on top.

"He did it! My baby won!" I scream, again causing all eyes to be on us, but who cares? We're used to being the black sheep in the crowd—literally. I can't wait to hug and kiss my boo.

"That wasn't nearly as boring as I thought it was going to be," Mickey says while she and Nigel clear the table. Chance and I finished cleaning our trash and are waiting for Jeremy to come over and get his props.

"Boring? Girl, please. This is sportsmanship at its finest: a man, a board, and the sea. There's nothing like it." Chance's nostalgia goes over both our heads. Nigel loves sports and feels his boy but personally, I don't understand how anyone could want to get in the ice-cold water for any amount of time, especially with sharks and jellyfish out there that can kill a sistah quick. I'm cool with cheerleading.

"Hey, I'm glad you guys could make it," Jeremy says, approaching our table. I jump into Jeremy's arms before anyone else gets to congratulate my man.

"Hey, man, you were pretty bad-ass out there," Chance says, giving him a high five.

"Yeah, man, you really did your thing," Nigel says, shaking Jeremy's hand as we walk to the table. "I hate to rush out, but Mickey and I have Lamaze class in an hour."

"Good job, white boy," Mickey says, punching Jeremy in the arm. Jeremy snickers at Mickey's comment, now used to the way she rolls. Mickey's a lot to handle on a good day, and a hurricane on a bad one. "See you later, Jayd. And thanks again for the balm."

"No problem, Mickey. See y'all later," I say to my friends, glad we're all okay again for the time being. As they walk toward their car, Alia walks up, headed straight for Chance.

"Hey, guys," Alia says, giving me a big hug. "Good job out there, Jeremy."

"Thanks," Jeremy says, holding me tightly now that I'm back in his arms. I watch Chance eyeing Alia, who is a very attractive girl and she has a kind heart, not to mention brains. She's a little shorter than Chance, but much taller than me, with long blond hair hanging down to her butt. Alia returns the look, smiling at Chance and blushing: White girls can't hide when they're feeling a guy, like a sistah can.

"What are you doing here?" I ask Alia, trying to break up the obvious energy between her and my friend. Even if Nellie's being a bitch right now, I don't feel comfortable watching her boyfriend flirt with another girl in my presence.

"My brother's on one of the other surf teams. They came in second," Alia says, still looking at Chance. This girl's got it bad, and from what I can see, Chance is catching the fever, too. "We're all going to hang out at my house. Are you guys coming?" Alia's asking all of us but only talking to one person.

"I'm actually not up for a big party in Palos Verdes tonight, but, Jeremy, if you want to hang out with your friends, I can respect that. You deserve to party, baby," I say, looking up at my man. He looks damn good in his black wet suit with his bushy brown curls all over his head, kissed by all the sun they've been getting due to his hectic surf schedule this past month.

"Jayd, please. There's no party without you," Jeremy says, bending down to kiss me on the nose. I love being in love with someone who loves me right back. "I'm starving. Let me hit the showers real quick and grab my stuff. Then we can grab some dinner. Later, and tell your bro I said good surf," Jeremy says to Alia and Chance, who look like they're already having a good time.

"Have fun," I say to Chance and Alia as they stroll off toward the pre-party by the water. Nellie better get on her A game or she's going to be dropped like a hot biscuit. I don't blame Chance if he does leave Nellie on the sidelines, with the way she's been acting lately. Life's too short for tripping broads and, like Chance, I'm all for enjoying the moment. And right now, my man's calling me to come over to where his car's parked, and I'm ready to enjoy the ride.

Much to both our pleasures, Jeremy and I decide on our all-time favorite pizza spot off Manhattan Beach Boulevard. It's packed this afternoon, but that's a given. It's a beautiful day, and outside is the best place to be.

"Congratulations, honey. This one's on me," I say, pulling out my wallet and paying for Jeremy's food. He looks at me like he's seeing something straight out of *Guinness World Records.* I guess he's never had a girl insist on paying.

"Jayd, I told you, girl. Your money's no good with me." Jeremy tries to take his wallet out but the cashier, completely unfazed by our cuteness, takes the twenty out of my hand and pays the bill. That settles that.

"And I've got the movie, too, so don't even try it when we get to the theater," I say, smiling big as all outdoors. It feels good to be able to treat my man sometimes. It's not often that I can afford to feed anyone else, but because of my extra tips this week and the money Mama gave me for helping her fill some of her clients' orders, I'm doing okay. I also had several clients last night and this morning, putting me over the threshold for my half of Mama's stove. She'll be a little upset at first that I spent the money, but then she'll get over it, just like Jeremy.

"Has anyone ever told you you're pushy, Miss Jackson?" Jeremy asks, taking the plastic cups and lids from the cashier and leading the way to the soda machine.

"This is a special occasion, Jeremy. Besides, can't I treat

my man sometimes?" Not to mention I feel guilty about all the hell I've wreaked on him lately. Between my dreams and the drama with Rah, we've been going through it.

"Yes, you can," Jeremy says, bending his tall frame down to meet my tiptoed stance. We kiss for what seems like forever as we wait for our food. I can feel all eyes on us, but I don't care. We're in love and the haters can hate if they want to. Jeremy and I've missed hanging and I'm looking forward to a summer full of days like this.

"Aren't you two a sight for sore eyes?" Tania says, interrupting our public display of affection and leading her rich-girl crew into the quaint pizza joint. I guess once an alpha bitch, always one. She's dressed in the finest maternity clothes money can buy. I have to admit, the Persian princess looks cute pregnant, even if she is way too young to be a model for *Motherhood*. Because of Mickey I know way too much about the latest in maternity fashion.

"Tania," Jeremy says, his olive complexion turning the whitest I've ever seen at the sight of his baby-mama and her bulging stomach entering the building. I knew the day would come when Jeremy would have to acknowledge his impending fatherhood, but I didn't think it would be today. Jeremy takes a deep breath, leaning against the cool metal rail framing the drink bar. I reach for the cups and lids before he forgets they're in his hands.

"Hi, Jeremy," Tania says, obviously pleased with the level of discomfort Jeremy's in. Laura and the rest of the girls spot a booth and take a seat well within earshot. I know they want to witness this reunion, and I'm not going anywhere either. I fill our cups and wait for the next move.

"So, how's everything going?" Jeremy asks, obviously nervous, although I'm not sure why. He folds his tanned bare arms across his chest, bracing himself.

"Very well. I love New York City. The fashion, the nightlife—

everything is so exciting," Tania says, but I'm wondering what kind of nightlife an eight-and-a-half-month-pregnant eighteen-year-old can really have. "The weather's a bit harsh, but my husband's taking very good care of me." Something about Tania's answer makes me uneasy. I know she's lying, but why? While she and Jeremy continue their falsely polite conversation, I'm going to probe her mind to see what I can find out, if she'll let me in.

"That's good to hear. I'm glad it's all working out for you," Jeremy says. I can hear both regret and relief in his voice. I'll worry about him later. Right now, Tania's thoughts are my main concern. I place our drinks down next to the bar, moving over so the other customers can fill their cups and so I can have a better view of Tania.

I focus on Tania's dark brown eyes, noticing her freshly threaded thick brows in the process. This girl must be more expensive to maintain than a Rolls-Royce. The diamond solitaire earrings in her lobes make it easier for me to cool her mind. Mama says certain stones carry certain vibrations and the clear ones are of the most assistance for our line of work, giving calm vibes to both the possessor and practitioner. Tania's mind is now completely cool, allowing me easy access and I'm in.

As she thinks of what to say next, I catch Tania's thoughts before they become words. She wants to tell Jeremy she's sorry about how this all went down, that her husband is boring, controlling, and never home. She hates her life in New York but does love the city, even if she's all alone on a good day and stuck with her rude in-laws on a bad one. She wants to come back home, but it's not an option for her. And worst of all—per her marriage agreement—as soon as their son is born, she has to have another baby for her husband. Now instead of slightly envying Tania, I actually feel sorry for her. At least she had more choices when she was a high school student. Now, Tania's being forced into a world of motherhood and wifehood way too soon.

"So, how long are you visiting for?" Jeremy asks, looking down at her belly and back at me. This is making my man feel very awkward, but Tania's the one in pain.

"I'm not sure," Tania says, giving me a look of pure disdain, even with me inside of her mind like I am. She's checking out my bebe sandals—one of my first gifts from Jeremy—Apple Bottoms jeans and simple yellow wifebeater, sizing me up. She's wondering what Jeremy could possibly see in a hood girl like me. Focusing on the neat cornrows hanging over my shoulders, Tania looks into my eyes, noticing me staring back at her. I see her envy of me all too clearly. Now I wish I didn't know what I know. That's the thing about my mom's powers: Sometimes I get more than I bargain for. Talk about being careful what you wish for. Tania and I both have that flaw in common.

"You're back here for good?" Jeremy's question is more of a plea, and we all know it. If his child were living around the corner it would be impossible for them to pretend like it isn't his. Jeremy's father has already made it clear that there are no brown babies allowed at their family reunions, so having his illegitimate child nearby would cause a lot of friction in their household, guaranteed.

"Oh, don't get your Birkenstocks in a bunch, Jeremy. I'm only going to be here to deliver the baby, since my husband's out of town on business," Tania says, showing off her rocks for all to see. That's quite a wedding band set for a young girl. It must be nice. If Mickey were here she'd flip out, and Nigel wouldn't hear the end of it. "My entire family is here and I wanted to come home where I'd have some help," Tania says, rubbing her stomach like Mickey does. Her girls look at her, then at each other, realizing they might be called upon to help out, too, and I know they're not feeling that at all. Tania looks back at her friends, who immediately look out the window and then back at Jeremy and me, envious of our relationship. As if I didn't have enough resident haters on deck, now this broad is back to help the cause. I'm sure Nellie and Misty will be pleased with the new addition to their "I hate Jayd" sorority.

"Number fifty-nine," the cashier says, finally calling our number. Grateful for the relief, Jeremy walks back to the counter, hands the cashier our receipt and grabs our tray after thanking her. I gently ease out of Tania's mind, refocusing my attention on my date, but not before I catch Tania daydreaming about what it would be like if she and Jeremy were still together. No, this heffa isn't still feeling my man.

"You look great," I say to Tania, who hasn't taken her eyes off me but has said nothing to me yet.

"I would say the same thing about you, Jayd, but lying isn't good for the baby," Tania says, smiling. I don't want to slap a pregnant chick, but I will if need be. I don't need to read her mind to see that she wishes her life was as simple as she assumes mine to be. I wouldn't call my path easy, but at least I don't have a husband and a kid to worry about—as if. Tania and Mickey have surely got that bitch thing down pat. I hope in both their cases it wears off with the delivery because if it doesn't, they're both going to have a hard time getting help from their friends. Family may have to stick by them, but we don't.

"You want to eat outside?" Jeremy asks, obviously ready to leave this uncomfortable scene behind, and so am I. I already know the real deal with Tania, and like the credit card commercial says, that's priceless.

"Yeah, that sounds good." I reclaim our drinks and walk toward the front door, winking at Tania as we head outside.

She can hate all she wants, but I've got the life she wishes she still had and the man, too. It's hard to feel too much sympathy when the broad makes it so easy to hate her.

"See you around, Tania," Jeremy says, taking one last glance at his unborn child before following me out the open double doors. "And good luck with the delivery and all. If you need anything, you know where to find me."

"Whatever," Tania says, sitting in the booth with her girls. She's trying to put on a brave front, but I know she wants to cry. What did she expect? Did Tania really think that she and Jeremy would be able to get back together after all that's happened? Tania didn't even bother to tell him she was pregnant until after her parents found her a husband to make it all legit in their eyes. And I don't know what Laura has been telling her about Jeremy and me, but we're solid and not going anywhere anytime soon. Not to sound mean, but I already lost one dude to an ex-girlfriend who happens to have his child, and I'll be damned if the same thing happens with us.

"Are you okay, baby?" I ask, sitting across from Jeremy at the only available table on the small outdoor patio. With the weather being warm, there are more people eating outside than in.

"Yeah, I'm fine. Just a little shook up, that's all. And hungry," he says, taking one of the four large slices and folding it in half before stuffing the pizza into his mouth. I'm hungry, too. "Thanks for being so cool about everything, Jayd," he says, adjusting his mouth to the hot food without taking a break in his eating.

"We all have shit, Jeremy." We do, but I don't want to talk about it.

After a few moments of quiet eating, Jeremy finishes the last slice of his pepperoni while I'm still on my first piece. He eyes my barbeque chicken slice and smiles. I guess surfing really works up an appetite.

"'Bye, you two," Tania says, with her followers leading the way into the busy parking lot, ruining our vibe. Laura's driving her new Mercedes-Benz, slightly inciting the hater in me. These broads around here know nothing about hard work.

The four girls pile into the cute ride with Tania carefully squeezing into the front seat. Her girls look at her, the two in the back holding the pizza and snickering at her large form. I can see the humiliation on Tania's face and it only makes me feel more sorry. But before I can get out the sympathy violin, Tania shoots me an evil glare, slamming the door.

"I should give her a one-finger wave, but I'm too much of a lady for that," I say, picking up my root beer and taking a big gulp, which results in an even bigger belch. "Excuse me," I say, making Jeremy laugh. He thinks my body functions are cute. Unfortunately I don't share the sentiment for his or anyone else's, but I'm glad he accepts me just like I am.

"Jayd, don't worry about her front. There's no replacing the real thing," Jeremy says, reassuring me like the good boyfriend he is. We finish our food and decide it's time to catch the show. My phone vibrates with a text from Rah asking me to braid his hair tomorrow morning. I quickly text him back letting him know he's on my calendar.

"Tell Rah I said hey," Jeremy says, throwing salt in my work game. And how did he know it was Rah?

"It's not like that," I say, feeling the need to defend myself. "He wants me to do his hair, that's all." And Rah's a paying client who always gives good tips. I have to keep business separate from pleasure. I hope Jeremy can learn to understand.

"I'm sure he doesn't see it that way." I can see Jeremy's

not giving this up anytime soon. I have to do something, and fast, to keep this afternoon from going completely sour.

"It's just like you said a minute ago, Jeremy," I say, trying to lighten the mood. "There's no substitute for the real thing. And we are the real thing, baby, no matter who's in our past," I say, rising from my seat and walking around the table to sit on his lap. I kiss Jeremy on the forehead, the nose, and then his lips, gently attempting to melt away his frustration. Some tricks a girlfriend knows without having to use psychic powers to chill her man out.

I know Jeremy's torn about not being in his child's life. He's already set up a trust fund for the baby and has money sent to Tania automatically every month, whether she wants it or not. In Jeremy's eyes, he's doing the most responsible thing he can. But I know part of him wants more. There's no replacing being there on a regular basis. I already went through that with Rah, and he's spent every day since being back in his daughter's life attempting to make up for that lost time. That's the only hold Sandy's got over him, and Tania has the same thing on Jeremy.

"But this is different, Jayd, and you know it. Rah has this power over you that I don't get." Jeremy shifts, trying to push me off his lap, but I'm not going anywhere.

"That's not entirely false, but it's not the truth, either." I know that sounded wrong, but it's how I feel. "It's like Hamburger Helper," I say, attempting to again bring some much-needed comic relief to the conversation. "Will it fill me up? Yes. Is it convenient? Most definitely. But is it the best thing for me? Not even close," I say, kissing Jeremy and causing the people around us to talk.

"So you're saying that Rah's the equivalent of Hamburger Helper and I'm what—chopped liver?" Jeremy's so cute even when he's being a smart-ass.

"No. I'm saying that both Tania and Rah are bad for us,

and that we, together, are all the healthy nourishment we need." I think I'm starting to bring Jeremy back to the middle.

"So if we're all we need, then no more Rah, right?" Where is all of this possessiveness coming from? When Jeremy and I first met, he was one of the most secure dudes I'd ever met. Now this Rah thing has got him bugging out.

"I can't lie, Jeremy. He's a part of my life, but I'll never cheat on you. You're stuck with me whether you like it or not," I say, kissing him on one cheek then the other, forcing a smile.

"Ditto, Lady J." Jeremy touches the gold bangle he bought me months ago and then looks up at my birthday gift from Rah. Shit. Now we're going back down, and I can't have that.

"We are supposed to be enjoying your victory, not sulking in regret." I bet now he's wishing he'd gone ahead and gotten as high as possible with his surfer buddies instead of choosing to celebrate with me. I'm bringing his victory high down, and running into Tania didn't help. "It's your night, baby, and I'm your girl, so stop tripping." Jeremy kisses my nose, then my lips, softly at first and then it turns into one of the most passionate kisses he's ever given me, and I forget all about the fact that we're outside.

"Let's get out of here," Jeremy says, expressing my sentiments exactly.

"I'm right behind you, baby." We toss our trash into the bin, ready to leave the restaurant and its drama behind in exchange for a celebratory Saturday night. Being in a real relationship is hard work, but quite rewarding when we're on the same page. I hope Jeremy feels I'm worth the work because I know he is. I'd rather be with my man over Rah any day, and I intend to make sure Jeremy knows it.

~ 8 ~
Growing Pains

*"I want to be your friend /
not now and then, but until the end /
. . . I'd rather be with you."*

—Bootsy Collins

When Jeremy and I woke up this morning after a wonderful night celebrating yesterday's victory, he prepared a quick breakfast for us and then we went on with our separate days. Jeremy's going to catch up on his sleep and I'm working, as usual.

It's been a while since I've had the pleasure of braiding Rah's hair; he relaxes at my slightest touch. I take the black plastic comb and part his hair in half. Rah's hair is so thick I don't need to use clips to hold the loose parts in place or on the ends of his braids. The comb won't move as long as Rah stays still.

"Have you been using my coconut oil blend for your scalp?" I ask, doing a careful survey of the work ahead of me. Rah hasn't been taking the best care of his hair, and he knows he can't lie to me about it. Whatever novice he's had up in his hair has not done his crown justice and has just made my job that much more difficult. Now I have to undo whatever she's done before I can work my magic.

"Nah, I ran out. I meant to ask you for some more, but I forgot," Rah says, resting his shoulders on my thighs. I need to start making him sit in a chair like all of my other clients, but I'm actually grateful to be sitting down while working, for a change.

"You can't forget to use the proper ingredients if you plan on keeping your head healthy, Rah," I say, vigorously scratching the dandruff patches dominating his once flawless terrain. Even with our issues, as Rah's stylist I have an obligation to keep his hair healthy. Otherwise, how does that make me look? "You can take the rest of this container after I'm done with it. And when you run out, I know Simply Wholesome has something all natural you can use until I get you some more," I say, reminding him the natural restaurant and grocery market is up the street from his house. Sometimes I miss working there, just for the employee discount. I haven't been back recently but should check on my former coworkers soon.

"I know, you're right. Good looking, Jayd." Rah allows my comb to heal his head in more ways than one as I lull him into complete submission with my technique. I carefully work through his head, scratching and soothing the tender spots with my oil, eventually massaging his entire scalp before weaving in the cornrows to replace the afro he's been rocking for the last month. I hope he recognizes that my skills are irreplaceable, whether we're getting along or not. Money is the business and I'm a professional. If I can braid up the thugs on the block, I can take care of my boy, even if he's an ass sometimes.

As I finish up the last braid, ready to add the final touch of my new finishing lotion onto my masterpiece, I hear Sandy walking into the quiet house and ruining our peaceful vibe. Shit. I'd hoped I'd be done before the broad got back. I have two more clients this afternoon and no time for her drama.

"Rah, I know you can hear me," Sandy yells through the front door. "I need help with these groceries and for you to come get your daughter. She's been working my goddamn nerves all day." Rah shakes awake in my lap, jumping up at her last comment. I know toddlers are a lot to handle, but in my experience Rahima's always a pleasure to have around.

"Stop cussing around Rahima, Sandy. Damn," he says, unconsciously doing the same thing, even if Rahima's in the other room. Rah wipes his eyes before walking to the wall mirror and checking out his immaculate do. His smile says it all. My job here is done.

"That'll be forty dollars, please," I say, packing up my tools before Sandy can switch her way back here. The less I see of that broad, the better. Hopefully I'll get to hug baby girl before I go, but not if I have to go through her mama to do it.

"Since when?" Rah asks, taking two folded twenty-dollar bills from his back pocket and handing them to me. "I'm your boy, remember? I thought you couldn't charge me over twenty dollars?"

"Times are hard," I say, leaving the remaining coconut oil blend on his desk next to his latest music projects. I miss kicking it in his studio, but ever since Sandy's arrival all of that has changed. Rah's house has become tainted by his baby-mama's energy, and our entire crew's feeling the repercussions. When we don't hang out at Nigel's place it's always at some public location.

"Well, in that case, here's an extra ten for the recession," Rah says, handing me two more five-dollar bills with a smile, and I gladly take the tip.

"Didn't you hear me calling you?" Sandy says, entering the den through the open kitchen door. Speak of the devil in the tight blue dress, leaving very little to the imagination. Where did she go grocery shopping, Hos "R" Us? "Oh, it's you again," Sandy says, almost snarling she's so pissed. I've learned to park up the block just in case the heffa wants to get creative with her keys on my car. Rahima runs past her evil mother and straight into my arms and I welcome the hug.

"Funny, I was thinking the same thing," I say, returning Sandy's evil glare.

"Whatever," she says, refocusing her attention on Rah. "I need to get this food on for Rahima before I go to work, so you need to get the rest of the groceries out of the car," Sandy says, waving a box of Hamburger Helper and a pound of ground beef in the air. I just had a conversation about that food product last night and I know Rah's not feeling giving his baby that.

Even with his father in prison for at least twenty years, Rah still abides by the strict Muslim diet he and his little brother, Kamal, grew up on. Too bad his ghost of a mother doesn't feel the same, leaving Rah and Kamal to fend for themselves. Luckily, Rah does most of the grocery shopping and cooking for the household since his mother's rarely home.

"That's not food, and you're not feeding that crap to my daughter," Rah says, following Sandy into the kitchen. This is definitely my cue to leave. I wish I could take Rahima with me, but I have no claim to this little girl, no matter how much I love her. I kiss her on the forehead one more time before putting her down. I have a couple of hours before my next client and could use some lunch myself.

"Well, I need to fix her something quick because I've got to be at work in twenty minutes, so unless you have a better idea, this is it," Sandy says, in full bitch stance. It's sad to say, but I hope Rahima grows up to be nothing like her mother.

"I'll feed her, Sandy. Don't worry about it," Rah says, taking out all the makings for a healthy breakfast. "You go on to work. And tell my mama that she's got mail here, if she cares." Looking satisfied but surprised, Sandy walks out of the kitchen, leaving us alone again. How Rah deals with his mother and Sandy both working at the same strip club and driving him crazy is beyond me.

"Fine. I'm out," Sandy says, slamming the door without even saying good-bye to her daughter.

"I'm sorry about that, Jayd," he says, picking up his daughter and hugging her tightly. He lets her down and she runs straight over to me. I pick her up, happy for more hugs and notice her hair is also in need of some desperate attention, much like her daddy's was before I hooked him up.

"You mind if I do her hair real quick? I've got a little time to kill," I say, running my hand over the baby's tangled tresses. Mama would have a fit if she saw this child's neglected head.

"Be my guest," Rah says, cracking eggs into a mixing bowl and getting it started in the kitchen. I know he'll feed me, too.

I can already see the cornrows I'd like to braid in Rahima's head. If all goes well, she'll be asleep in my lap before I finish the first braid. But that's a long way off. I need to give her hair a good washing and conditioning, and oil her scalp.

"I'm going to need the rest of that oil after all," I say, heading back into the studio with Rahima. I can wash her hair in the tub back here and really give her hair the proper attention it deserves.

"Damn, I've got to make a run real quick after I finish cooking," he says, checking his texts. "You mind if I leave y'all here? I'll be right back." Rah's famous last words. Part of his weed hustling is being on-call like a doctor. I'll be so glad when he finds another hustle.

"Not a problem. As long as you leave the food," I say, taking my hair tools back out of the bag and setting up shop again. I turn the television to PBS and one of my favorite kids' cartoons is on.

"*WordGirl!*" Rahima screams with a big smile on her face. The girl's got good taste. Next to *The Powerpuff Girls,* this is my favorite cartoon.

"I see y'all are set," Rah says, placing two plates of bis-cuits, eggs, veggies, and turkey bacon on the table in front of us. He kisses Rahima on the cheek, wanting to show me the same affection, but he knows not to go there with me any-more. We hug and he's out.

"It's just you and me, kid," I say to a smiling Rahima, who's already digging into her plate. The fork's almost big-ger than her mouth, but that doesn't stop her from eating. She's my kind of girl. Before I know it she'll be cooking us breakfast. I hope her daddy grows up with her and leaves all this street shit behind—crazy baby-mamas, illegal employ-ment and all. Rah can do so much better. I know it's going to hurt him financially for a while, but sacrifice is a large part of growing up, and it's time for us all to cut out the bull so we can thrive.

After finishing our lunch and Rahima's hair, I put Rahima down for a nap and lie on the futon, hoping to doze off for an hour before I have to get back to work. Before I can get too comfy, there's a knock at the door. I try to leave it be since this isn't my house, but whoever it is is persistent, and I have no choice but to answer, even if it's against my better judgment. I look through the peephole and then open the door. They really should consider getting a security screen.

"Hello. I'm looking for Sandy," an uptight-looking white guy says. "I'm her parole officer, here to check on her." If he didn't tell me who he was, I would've thought him to be a lost salesman of some sort. There aren't many white people on this side of LA.

"She's at work," I say. Ain't this some shit? The one day I'm here and she's not, this dude decides to show up. What the hell?

"Well, can you give her this for me, please? She has to be in court on Monday. I've been trying to reach her, but she's not returning my calls and she hasn't come in for her weekly appointments all month," he says, holding out an envelope. What kind of parole officer is he? With all of those offenses, shouldn't Sandy be back in jail by now?

"Why don't you give it to her yourself. I don't know Sandy like that," I say, refusing to be a part of the trick's world any more than I have to be. And taking responsibility for her mail is more than I'm willing to do.

"Don't you live here?" he asks. I guess he thinks all black people live in houses with a lot of people. That's true for most of the folks I know in Compton, but he still shouldn't feel comfortable assuming.

"No. I'm just a friend of her daughter's father. This is his house, not hers," I say, ready to close the door and resume my nap.

"Oh, I see," he says, looking around, confused. "I thought she—and Raheem, is it?" he says, stumbling over Rah's full first name.

"Yes, it is."

"I was under the impression that they were engaged, and that Sandy would be living here permanently."

"Say what?" I ask as Rah pulls up in the driveway, just in time to set the record straight. Somebody's been lying big-time, and I have a feeling he knows nothing about this one, or at least I hope not. Noticing the white man on his porch, Rah jumps out of his Acura with a concerned look on his face. He probably thinks he's a cop.

"What's up, Jayd?" Rah asks, stepping onto the front porch in full defense mode.

"I'm Tucker Benton, Sandy's parole officer. You must be her fiancé, Raheem." The shocked look on Rah's face says it all. He knew nothing about Sandy's latest stunt.

"Her what?" Rah looks from Tucker to me, dazed and confused. Even though she rarely wears much clothing, Sandy's always got something up her sleeve. "Look, man, we have a kid together and I'm letting her serve her parole out here, but that's it. Sandy and I haven't been together in years."

"Well, I'm sorry for the confusion, but I am concerned. According to her ankle bracelet, she's been coming in past her approved curfew. Because of her chosen profession we've been lenient, but I can't continue to let her get away with this type of negligence." Chosen profession? No one chooses to be a stripper as an occupation. They kind of just fall into it—literally.

Tucker hands Rah the envelope he tried to push off on me, officially serving Sandy through Rah.

"She needs to be in court with a good explanation Monday morning. Good day," he says, walking back to his car parked across the street. Rah looks at the mail in his hand and up at me, embarrassed and pissed.

"Sorry about that, Jayd," Rah says, following me back inside and closing the door behind us. "How's Rahima?"

"She's fine. Napping on a full stomach and fresh hairdo," I say. "Where did Sandy get the idea that you two were tying the knot?" I ask. Even if she was way off base, I want to make sure Rah's telling the whole truth and nothing but the truth, so help him Jayd.

"Girl, I don't know," he says, walking to the studio door and checking on his baby. I follow him through the kitchen, seeing the same thing he does: a contented little girl knocked out on the futon, where I should still be. He turns around, wrapping his arms around my waist like I'm still his girl. "You know if I was going to wife anyone up, it would be you," he says, attempting to kiss my neck, but I'm not having it. I promised my man I wouldn't let Rah touch me, and here we are again.

"Look, Rah, you can't be all up on me like that. You know I have a boyfriend."

"What the white boy doesn't know won't hurt him." Rah

holds me tighter, now trying to kiss me on the lips. I smack him hard on the chest and wiggle away from him.

"This is exactly why we need to keep things strictly business between us from now on. If you need your hair done again, holla. Otherwise, we can't be alone together anymore." Rah smiles at my declaration, letting me go. I pass him up, grab my hair bag and purse, and head for the door. I've got to get back to my mom's house before my clients arrive.

"No matter how many boyfriends you have or fiancées I get, it'll always be me and you, girl, 'til the end," he says to my back as I walk out the front door. Rah has an uncanny ability to get in my head and heart, but we need to grow up and get over it.

Rah was my first love in junior high school, back in the day. I'm seventeen now and so is he, but we still act like the two twelve-year-olds who first fell in love at Family Christian many years ago. If Nigel hadn't transferred to South Bay High this year, Rah and I would have never been friends again after I found out he and Sandy—my former best friend— were having a baby. Why he's reappeared in my life, I'm not sure. But I have to do the mature thing and keep my distance from him before I ruin the good thing Jeremy and I have got going. When Jeremy comes over tonight, I'm going to tell him a million times how much I love him and try my damnedest to stay away from Rah from now on.

My hands were so sore from braiding yesterday that cooking dinner was out of the question. Jeremy picked us up some Chinese food and we stayed in and caught up on our days before passing out in the living room. I love having Jeremy around and am so glad his busy surf schedule is over. I missed hanging with my man on a daily basis.

It's been a quiet Monday so far, but that's about to

change. With the rehearsals for the spring play in full effect this week, I'll have less time than usual to hang with my dilapidated crew, and for that I am grateful. Nellie still hates me for making the cheer squad when I had nothing to do with the final decision making, and she knows that. But whatever. I'm tired of holding back my own progress because my friend has issues with me spreading my wings. If Nellie can't be happy for my growth, that's on her. I'm here to shine and that's exactly what I'm going to do, with or without her enthusiasm.

Speaking of which, I haven't called my dad to thank him for sending my birthday card, and that was over a month ago. I guess I should be a big girl and say thank you, even if he only sent twenty dollars to accompany it. I'm not spoiled or anything, but I think I deserve more than that from my father for my seventeenth birthday. Mama always says I shouldn't be ungrateful, and I'm trying. It's just part of growing up to be the bigger person, so here goes nothing.

I scroll down to my daddy's contact on my cell and press Send. I'm half hoping he lets it roll to voice mail, but he picks up, beginning the awkward conversation my father and I always have.

"This is Carter Jackson," he says, like he can't see my name on his caller ID. My dad can be so weird sometimes.

"And this is Jayd Jackson," I say, returning the formal greeting. "Hi, Daddy. Thank you for the birthday card," I say, the first to break the ice. He always thinks I'm calling for money, but I stopped begging from him a long time ago. Working hard has its benefits. One is definitely the satisfaction of being financially independent.

"Hey, baby," my daddy says, seemingly happy to hear from me. "I was starting to wonder whether it and the money I sent got lost in the mail," he says, like it was a hundred-dollar bill. "How's my youngest daughter doing?"

"I'm well," I say, readjusting my backpack on my shoulders as I make my way out of the parking lot toward my Spanish class. I don't mind being early for any class Mr. Adewale's teaching. "How's Faye?" I ask, noticing the seagulls circling above my head in the open sky. I'd better get to one of the covered picnic tables before they start dropping white bombs all over the place. So far this year Mickey's the only one of my friends who's suffered that humiliating event, but that luck can change at any time.

"She's good, working hard," he says. "When's the last time you've been to the dentist or the eye doctor?" my father asks, all up in my business this morning. Since when does he care about my physicals? I locate a safe, covered spot to continue my morning conversation and take my backpack off. This thing can get heavy when I'm walking around.

"I don't know, Daddy. Since my mom took me last, I guess." And who knows when that was. Unless I'm having some sort of pain, I don't get regular trips to the doctor, especially if it involves my mom having to take time out of her busy social schedule or time off work. I have to be near death just to go to the pediatrician.

"Well, Miss Jackson, that won't fly anymore," my daddy says, clearing his throat. He loves calling me by my last name because it's his name, too. I guess Jayd reminds him too much of my mom and Mama. "You're a big girl now, and you can drive yourself to your appointments." I never thought of that. I guess I could technically be responsible for my own well-being, but that's not on my itinerary, either, even if my vision has been a little blurry.

"Daddy, I've got too much to do, and besides, the eye doctor and dentist are all the way in Long Beach. That's too far for me to drive, even if it's not rush hour traffic."

"Girl, your stepmother and I work hard for those benefits, and you're going to use them or get kicked off," my dad says, threatening me. But I already know my medical benefits are a part of the custody agreement he and my mom agreed on when they got divorced, so his threat is empty, but I hear him. I need to take better care of myself, especially while I've got access to his benefits. I know he'll bump me off as soon as he can.

"Well, can I at least get switched to a dentist and optometrist closer to home?" I ask, realizing the school bell should be ringing any minute now. Usually I wouldn't be in a rush to get my day started, but I would gladly welcome any interruption to this conversation.

"No. You can go where we all go. You've still got your mother's car, right? Or has she taken it back already?" It's funny how my dad always thinks the worst of my mom, but he's the one doing all the hating. Go figure.

"Yes, Daddy. But gas and time cost money that I don't have," I say, alluding to the fact that he doesn't pay my bills, even if technically he should. I love it that my grandfather gives me gas money whenever he sees me; it makes a girl feel special and loved.

"What happened to your job? Did you quit doing hair already, girl?" He is so far off it's not even funny. My dad also doesn't know about me moving to my mom's and frankly, it's none of his business.

"No, Daddy. I still have my job." And my side business braiding hair, but he doesn't need to know that, either. "The point is that Long Beach isn't down the street, and because I work in Compton and go to school in Redondo Beach, I don't have the time to drive all the way there and back. Why can't I just switch it?" And why does he have to be so damned difficult? It was his idea for me to go, but now that I want to, it's too much. What the hell?

"Because you can't, that's why. Now call and make an appointment sooner than later," he says, in his usual demanding tone. I wonder if he's this mean to the car salesmen he manages. "Your stepmother and I get charged whether you go or not, so go." There's the first bell and right on time, too. Me and my daddy need to go to our separate corners and cool off before I snap.

"'Bye, Daddy," I say, more than ready to go. I have a lot to do today, including studying for my debutante meeting next weekend. I haven't memorized nearly as much as I need to. Mrs. Esop made it a point to politely scold me for my lack of knowledge about sorority history at the last meeting. At least it was in private because, like my daddy, she can be a bit much at times.

"'Bye, Jayd. Have a good day, you hear?" I return the well wishes and hang up the phone, looking around at the campus full of students and teachers alike. From where I'm seated, I can see the ocean clearly. I wish I were sitting on the beach listening to the waves, and not about to start my school day. If I didn't have an ASU meeting at lunch, I might find my way to the shore. But duty calls and I've got to answer, even when I don't necessarily want to.

The days become longer and more intolerable every day we get closer to summer. I'm grateful that I get to see Mr. Adewale twice a day, and three times when we have an ASU meeting, like now. Jeremy wanted to chill with me for lunch, but we'll have to wait until later to catch up. I'm actually looking forward to our first official meeting as officers. Ms. Toni's going to lay down the law today and pass out a list of our official duties while Mr. A discusses the school calendar for next year. I doubt that Chance will show up since he wasn't in fourth period. I know he's going through a lot, but he needs to suck it up and take his office of treasurer seriously. Otherwise, he's going to lose it before he even officially begins.

I step into the classroom with my lunch in hand, ready to grub and get on with this meeting. The sooner we get Monday over, the faster Friday will come. The only person present is Nigel, and it doesn't look like he ever left to get lunch like the other classmates who are also in ASU. I know he's hungry and I also know Mickey isn't the type to get her man's food—it's the other way around with her, so something else must be up. I walk over to my friend's desk and take the seat next to him, where his girl usually sits. I'll move when Mickey gets here. I hope she can appreciate me checking on my friend.

"Jayd, my mom wants you to call her when you get a chance. She needs to give you the new schedule for the debutante shit," Nigel says less than enthusiastically.

"What's up with the sour attitude today?" I ask, noticing how agitated Nigel is.

"Man, it's everything," Nigel says, putting his head in his hands. He looks like he wants to cry, but I know better than that. Brothas don't drop tears unless someone dies or they lose a game.

"You want to talk about it?" I ask. We've got about three minutes until the rest of the African Student Union members arrive. That's not much time, but it'll have to do.

"Jayd, I'm not ready for this," he says. I know he's not talking about the meeting, so it must be the baby. "My mom's been riding me all week about getting a job and shit, and you know I don't have time for that," he says, sharing his stress with me. I don't know what Nigel was thinking, taking on a baby, especially when he knows he's not the father. Talk about a reality check.

"Well, I'm sure there's something you can do that won't take up too much of your practice time," I say, putting my right hand on my boy's shoulder. I'm here for my friend like he's always here for me, even if I disagree with some of his recent decisions. Don't get me wrong—I think it's honorable the way Nigel's standing up for Mickey and Tre's baby, especially since Tre saved Nigel's life by sacrificing his own when Mickey's ex-man tried to shoot Nigel after he found out Mickey was cheating on him. But it's still not Nigel's responsibility to raise this child.

"Like what, Jayd? My mom's expecting me to be an escort at the ball, too, and God knows I don't want to do that shit again," Nigel says, again shaking his head in distress. "The baby's going to be here before we know it, and I don't even know where we're going to live. What the hell was I thinking?" Nigel's really feeling the heaviness of his chosen path this afternoon. Having a baby is more than a romantic notion. I guess when he thought they were all going to live under one roof and be a happy black family—like the Cosbys meet Reba—it was cool. But now that the baby is affirmatively not an Esop, his mom has laid down the law, and Mickey and her baby not being in the family was her first declaration.

"Does Mickey know about all of this?" I ask, wondering how much of his emotions Nigel shares with this girlfriend. They need to be as real with each other as possible, but too real might piss Mickey off.

"Nah, I'm afraid to tell her," Nigel says, looking into my eyes and I into his. "She's so scared about giving birth, and I don't want to trip her out about this. I told her we'd figure it out before the baby gets here, though."

"Well, that's sooner than later, my brotha," I say, focusing on Nigel's dark brown eyes, trying to jump into his mind and cool him off before the rest of the group arrives, which should be any minute now. Mr. Adewale and Ms. Toni went outside to chat and should return any minute as well. If Nigel could just step back from all of the emotions he's feeling, he might be able to gain some insight on what it is that he should do in everyone's best interest. He and Rah make good money from their side hustles, but because Nigel's an athlete, he doesn't hustle as hard as Rah does and his money from his parents is great for him, but not nearly enough to support a family.

"I know. Don't remind me," he says with a slight smile but more pain. "I can't believe she'll be here any day now." I focus on the darkness of Nigel's eyes, feeling his mind cool at my entrance. He's a tough one to crack, but I'm in.

I see Nigel's worry and frustrations clearly now, and also feel his pain and fear about taking on Mickey and her baby. I don't know how he felt before verifying the paternity, but now that it's Tre's baby, Nigel's feelings are mixed. He's grateful he dodged a bullet more than once, but now he's not sure he made the right decision taking the weight of Mickey's world on his shoulders. On one hand, he's happy the baby's not his and that he has another chance at getting it right next time, birth control included in his future plans. But on the other hand, Nigel wishes the baby were his so his parents would have helped out, no matter how displeased they would've been. Also, that way he would've had a concrete connection to the baby, which he fears he doesn't have now.

It's my job as Nickey Shantae's godmother to make sure that Mickey and Nigel get their acts together, and that's just what I intend to do, starting with Nigel stepping all the way up if he's willing to. If it weren't for that little baby speaking to me in a dream a few months ago when I tapped into Mickey's sleeping head, I would probably feel very torn about Nigel claiming Mickey and the baby, too. But we're past that now, and I have to get my boy to see things my way, and fast. Nigel doesn't have his running shoes on yet, but he's shopping for them.

"Nigel, you're a good brotha and you love Mickey and her

baby," I say aloud, watching as the words move from my mind to his. Nigel knows he's made the right choice but doesn't have the support he needs to walk his chosen path. That's what I'm here for.

"I do love Mickey and the baby, too," Nigel repeats, calming down as his mind clears. "I love them both and I'm going to take care of them." Right as we come to a psychic agreement, Mr. Adewale walks back in with the rest of ASU filing in, too. I release Nigel from my visual counseling session and turn my focus to our fine-ass teacher taking his place at the board.

"That's weird," Nigel says, blinking his eyes quickly and shaking his head. "I feel like my ears just popped or something." Some people are more sensitive to my mom's gift than others. I remember when cooling Jeremy off during an argument we had at Mickey's baby shower, he said he felt like he had a brain freeze. Chance's mother felt a similar sensation when I met her for the first time, trying to calm her hot ass down, too. I guess the aftereffects are different for everyone.

"Good afternoon, students," Mr. Adewale says, Ms. Toni making her grand entrance last and winking at me before she takes a seat behind the teacher's desk. They make a great team. Too bad Ms. Toni's not in the market for a much younger man. I wouldn't mind seeing the two of them together, but she's still mourning the tragic death of her husband years ago. To hear her tell it, all she has time for is her two daughters and her job.

Mickey waddles in, completely uncomfortable in her pregnant body. I feel for my girl, especially since the worst is still yet to come. She looks at me sitting in her seat and I can see the neck getting ready to roll. Before Mickey can say a word, Nigel rises to help his girl out.

"I love you, baby. You know I'd rather be with you any day.

I just want you to know that," Nigel says, bringing Mickey's hands up to his lips and kissing her knuckles. Mickey's tears fall on her shirt, wetting the delicate blue fabric. He then places his hand on Mickey's stomach and she puts her hand over his, letting them bond with their baby for a moment.

"Well, isn't that sweet," Misty says, late as usual. KJ and the rest of their crew take their seats as we finally begin our meeting. I wish Jeremy were here, but he opted to nap in the library. Lucky him. Hopefully we'll both get some good rest tonight. I wish I could slow down like Jeremy does when he feels like it, but a sistah's got too much work to do to simply stop. I've got to keep pushing if I plan on making it through the next six weeks of school, starting with making it through the rest of this week.

~ 9 ~
Pushin'

"How can I ignore?
This is sex without touching."

—Björk

*S*weat drops slowly make their way from the top of my
forehead down to my cheek, eventually landing on the
fresh white sheets. I'm panting heavily and the cramps in
my stomach are almost too much to bear.

"Ogunlabi, please help me," I say, reaching my hand out
to my husband for support. Mr. Adewale and I are again
married, like in another dream I had when we first met
months ago. The contractions are getting fiercer with each
passing moment. "The baby's coming!" I shout, more out of
excitement than fear.

"Okay, baby. It's going to be okay," he says, wiping my
brow with a cold towel and watching the midwife check me
out. He offers me ice chips, but I just want this to be over.

"It's time to push, Jayd," the midwife says, smiling up at
me. "The next time you feel a contraction, push down as
hard as you can."

"Like you're having a bowel movement," my mom says
from her mind to mine even though she's in the room with
us all. I guess she doesn't want to embarrass me, but it feels
like that's exactly what I'm supposed to do. I bear down
and push as hard as I can, causing my husband's hand as

much pain as I can in the process. Mr. A isn't complaining, like a good husband.

"Jayd, don't be afraid," Mama says, holding my left hand tightly and helping me stay focused on the goal, which is to push this baby out of me. "Trust your body to do what it does naturally. Stay calm and push." Taking both of my mothers' advice, I bear down and push again with all my might.

"Ogunlabi!" I yell at the shear thrust of the baby's head making its way into the world. "I can't take any more," I say, ready to give up. It's been a long, hard labor and I'm not sure that I can take any more, but I have to because we're not done yet.

"Jayd Jackson Adewale, bring our daughter into the world," my husband says, urging me to keep pushing. With him and Mama supporting me, I give it one more push and finally deliver my baby.

"It's a girl!" Netta, acting as the midwife, says, handing Mama the baby to clean off and look over before passing our daughter to me. Mama then replaces Netta as the midwife, cutting the cord and getting ready to prep the afterbirth for the spiritual ritual all babies in our religion receive, whether they have a caul or not, which my daughter clearly has.

"Look at her eyes," I say, staring at my daughter's green eyes looking back at me in amazement. "She's got our sight in more ways than one."

"I think we should name her after Maman," Mama says, allowing Netta to finish cleaning me up so Netta can hold Mama's great-grandbaby. "Marie Jayd Williams Adewale."

"I like the sound of that," I say, handing Mama the baby to give to Netta. Mr. Adewale hasn't held our daughter yet, and is apparently okay with that. He already knows how we women get down in the Williams clan, and wouldn't

*have it any other way. I repeat our daughter's name and
suddenly wake up.*

"What happened?" I say to Jeremy, who's looking at me
like I just farted loudly in my sleep. It wouldn't be the first
time, although he's never complained before. There's
enough of that to go around for both of us.

"Jayd Adewale, huh?" Jeremy says, throwing the covers off
us both before rising to his feet. Oh shit. I must've been talking in my sleep again. I hate when that happens, especially if
the witness isn't Mama.

"It was just a dream," I say, rising with him, still sluggish.
But Jeremy's too pissed for reason this morning. "I can't be
held accountable for shit that happens when I'm unconscious." I look around, noticing the sun's rising, but it's still
too early for us to be up, and on a Friday, too.

"The unconscious speaks volumes about what it is that
you really want, and who." Jeremy's visibly hurt by this
predawn revelation, but so off I can't even begin to explain it.

"Jeremy, that may be true in Freud's world, but my dreams
mean a lot more than that. Wait, that didn't sound right," I
say, realizing I'm not making the situation any better. "What I
mean is that my dreams are messages, Jeremy, and since I'm
not the one pregnant, I don't think it was about me at all."

"Whatever, Jayd. I've got to get going." Jeremy slips on his
Birkenstocks, unlocks the various bolts and chains on my
mom's front door and leaves, slamming the door shut behind him. Damn, this is not a good way to start our morning,
but it's here so I'll have to deal with it—and he's not getting
off that easy. I slip on my sandals, open the front door and
run down the stairs, catching Jeremy in the driveway.

"Jeremy, I keep having these dreams and I can't control
them. I'm sorry you have to witness them sometimes, but

there's nothing I can do. It's a part of my gift, Jeremy." He turns around at the end of the driveway, facing me. Jeremy looks so pissed he could punch a wall.

"I know that, Jayd," he says, cooling down a bit but not completely. "It's just a reaction, like your spontaneous dreams about other guys." It's not exactly the same thing, but I feel where he's coming from.

"Jeremy, I'm learning how to control my visions, but it's going to take some time," I say, walking up to him and holding his hands. Thank God summer's around the corner, providing warmer mornings. Otherwise we'd both catch a cold in the early morning chill. I'm trying to keep my voice low because most of my neighbors are still sleeping. There are a couple of lights on in the surrounding apartments, but most people don't rise until after the sun's completely up.

"So you're telling me that this dream is a result of you being a voodoo priestess? How does one have anything to do with the other?" Jeremy's blue eyes are sincere and I want to be able to tell him everything, but I don't know how or if I can.

I look down at Jeremy's ashy knuckles, caressing them with my thumbs. How can I make him understand my gifts? I lead him back toward the stairway to my mom's apartment and he follows. This is not a conversation I want to continue outside. Even if it is the wee hours of the morning, the walls around here have ears. I wouldn't be surprised if my next-door neighbor and client, Shawntrese, is listening at the door.

Once inside, we sit down on the cozy couch and face each other. I look into his eyes, focusing on the strain I feel coming from his mind, cooling his thoughts and allowing him to come to his own conclusion rather than influencing his mind.

"Every woman in my lineage has a gift of sight," I say, still locked onto his eyes. "My great-grandmother could cripple someone with her thoughts. My grandmother can use anyone's thoughts to her advantage. My mother lost her gift of sight, which was to cool a person's mind and make them see her point of view," I say, feeling his mind bend toward a clearer understanding of what I'm saying. "And my gift of sight comes in the form of dreams, Jeremy. Crazy, unpredictable, and mostly volatile dreams that I have no control over yet, but I'm working on it." I release my hold on Jeremy's vision, allowing him to adjust to the load I just laid on him.

"Wow, that's the second time I've felt like I had a brain freeze without drinking anything cold. What the hell?" he says, borrowing my coined phrase.

"Okay, now I have another confession to make," I say, scooting a little closer to him. I hope he stays chill after I tell him I've tapped into his mind. "That cold feeling is the after-effect of me relaxing your mind," I say, Jeremy's eyes again locked onto mine. "I retained my mom's lost powers in one of my dreams and have been learning how to use them ever since."

"Really?" he asks, more fascinated than angry. "Can you read my mind?"

"No, not at all," I laugh, realizing he's curious about my lineage. I'm grateful he's not angry with me for not telling him the truth sooner. "We can't do anything to or for a person without his or her consent. And I never use my sight for evil. I'm sorry I didn't tell you sooner, but it's not something I share."

"But I never gave you permission to enter my mind."

"Not verbally, but when I look into your eyes your mind submits to my visual request, allowing me to tap into your emotions and cool you off, like now." Jeremy looks like he doesn't believe me and that's okay. I know it will take time for him to adjust, much like it did Rah and Nigel when I first told them about my dreams in junior high. Whether or not they believe me is irrelevant. The most important thing is that we remain friends without judgment.

"So Mr. Adewale's not your dream guy?" Jeremy asks, bringing the conversation full circle.

"No, baby," I say, slightly untruthful in my words, but he doesn't need to know that. "You're all I need, and I'm sorry my dream made you upset. But, baby, sometimes you can't let your jealousy get the best of you," I say, now hugging my man. It feels good being honest with him, even if he doesn't believe it all.

"Jayd, it's okay. It's not your fault. Hey, if I was a girl I'd probably think Mr. Adewale was cute, too," Jeremy says jokingly. I playfully punch him in the thigh. "Hey, I'm just saying."

"Don't even play like that, Jeremy." He looks at me and kisses me gently, truly forgiving me and I him. Now this is the way to wake up and get this morning started right. "Let's get up, baby. It's still a school day," I say, feeling the heat of the sun's rays on my back through the blinds.

"Don't remind me," he says, unwillingly rising from the couch. "See you at school, babe." He exits the apartment again, leaving me to get ready for our day. That was a crazy dream, and what's worse is that I've retained some of the back pain and cramps from my fantasy labor. I hope Mickey's ready, because from the small taste I got, labor is not going to be easy.

Finally, Friday is here and the school day is almost over. I've never been so happy to see a weekend come. My plan is to get my braid on today after school. I'm working four hours at Netta's and then I've got two heads to braid when I get back to Inglewood. It's going to be a late night, but well worth it.

Now let's see how well I handle this cheer schedule. Starting with the pre-football season, we practice four days a week with games on Friday. With the majority of the practice during sixth period gym class, it's not so bad. It's the Friday games Mama's not going to like, and me neither. That's one of my busiest shop days, and I'm going to miss the money. In the meantime, I'd better enjoy my Fridays while I can.

"Let's get it started, ladies," Alicia says, calling the new and old cheer squad members together in the gym. We line up in four rows, ready to get our dance on. This is way better than weight lifting class.

"Look to your right and to your left. Then look in front of you and behind you. These are your sisters for the next year. Welcome, ladies," Shauna says, officially introducing us to one another for the first time. I look in all four directions and notice that with the exception of myself and one other younger sister in the freshman line, there are no other girls of any color on next year's squad. That shit is crazy, but I guess Mr. Adelizi will be glad to know I made the cut. The colleges should be very happy to know that I can play their game and win.

"So, let's get started on our first routine, which we will perform at the final pep rally for the year in a couple of weeks," Alicia says. "This will be your formal introduction to the rest of the campus. So get it right, ladies, and give it your all!"

Shauna, Alicia, and the other veteran cheerleaders run from the sidelines into the middle of the gymnasium floor, flipping and kicking as high as they can. They didn't say being an acrobat was a requirement. Are they always this excited? It's like they've each had two Red Bulls and coffee be-

fore coming to practice. I hope that's not a requirement. I
had enough coffee to last me a lifetime when studying for the
AP exams, though I do miss the study group. We're supposed
to start up again in the summer to study for the SATs, and I
am so grateful to again be included. Lord knows I need all
the help I can get.

"Jayd, step out and show us what you've got," Shauna
says, pushing Play on her iPod as the music blares loudly
through the gymnasium's mega speakers. It's cool that I get
to finish out cheer as my PE elective even if I don't officially
start until the fall. I could learn to love the perks of being in
the cheerleaders and athletes clique, even if I never thought
I'd be a part of this crew. Before I can get my grove on, Nellie, Laura, Misty, and the rest of the ASB bitch crew walk in
and take a seat in the bleachers. Some of the athletes, including Nigel, KJ, and his crew also join us. I didn't know practice
was open to the public, but I guess I'd better get used to people watching me dance.

"Jayd, routine," Shauna asks again, and this time, I'm
on it.

I step away from the varsity line, ready to get my groove
on when Chance, Mickey, and Jeremy step into the gym.
Damn, more spectators. Did everyone hear the music? I
begin the first part of the routine, expertly matching the beat
in one of my favorite old school songs. The senior cheerleaders
look at me and smile, impressed with their teaching skills
and my natural ability to dance.

"Push it real good, Jayd," KJ yells from the bleachers.
Chance and Jeremy both look up and shoot him a look, but
KJ couldn't care less. He's a star basketball player and knows
we'll see way too much of each other now that I have practice at the same time as him and will accompany the teams to
games and all of the other social duties that come with being
a cheerleader. But I do have to admit, this part is fun.

"Sarah, Lindsay, Molly, and Rachel. Jump in on eight," Shauna says, directing two of the other girls on the varsity squad to join in the routine. They catch it on the beat, but are less enthusiastic in their dancing than I am, and Shauna notices. "You're too tight, ladies! Loosen up!" The girls begin to move more, but still look stiff as boards compared to me. A lot of the moves are too sensual for them, I can tell. But none of them are too sexual, unlike some of the cheer moves I've seen at the high schools in my hood. Some of those girls might as well have sex right then and there the way they dance during half time.

"All right, ladies," Alicia says at the end of the first routine. "Now it's time to learn a new cheer. Get back in line and pick up your pom-poms. This is what it's all about." I wipe the sweat from my brow and wave at my man, who's smiling from ear to ear. Jeremy was shocked when I first told him about trying out, but I know he likes what he sees. Nellie and her associated student bitches, on the other hand, look as sour as lemons. Whatever.

"Okay, ladies. Just like in tryouts, when your captain calls out 'ready' you respond with 'okay' and a loud clap, got it?" Shauna says, shouting at the top of her lungs. We nod our heads, ready for our cue. "We're going to start with a basic offense cheer we use at every game to get our teams hyped. Ready?"

"Okay!" we shout, but it's Mickey who responds the loudest.

"Oh shit," Mickey yells from her seat in the bleachers, standing up and looking down. "I think my water just broke."

"I got you, baby," Nigel says, taking Mickey by the elbow and escorting her out of the gym.

"That's just gross," Laura says, turning her nose up at the natural sight. We all look toward the door, Nellie included. I look at Shauna and back at my friend, knowing what I have to do.

"I need to be with her," I say, turning in my pom-poms. The other girls look at me like I've lost my mind, leaving the first practice—but what can I say? My goddaughter's birth trumps pom-poms any day.

"Go ahead, Jayd. You can catch up on Monday," Shauna says. She's cool as hell. Too bad she's graduating. Otherwise I think we could've become real good friends.

"Nigel, wait up. I'm coming with y'all," I say, running over to the bleachers and grabbing Mickey's backpack before catching up to my friends. Jeremy and Chance follow me out of the gymnasium, all of us running toward our cars.

"Jayd, I can't go to the hospital with you, baby. I've got plans with my brothers after school," Jeremy says. "And I don't think it's my place anyway." What he's not saying is that he doesn't want to run into Rah, the baby's godfather, who he knows will be there by the time we arrive.

"Okay, baby. I'll call you later," I say, giving him a quick kiss before running to the main lot where my car is parked. I need to call my clients and let them know I won't be able to make it today, after I call Mama and Netta, of course. I can't believe she's finally coming. It feels like we've been waiting for Nickey Shantae to make her appearance forever, and now the day is here.

Poor Mickey. She's been in labor for several hours with barely any progress. It looks like it's going to be a long night, and Mickey and Nigel are prepared, with playing cards and plenty of hard candy for Mickey to suck on since she can't eat anything. I know she's in hell, but she's being a good sport so far.

It's been difficult seeing Rah all evening, too. I haven't talked to him since the run-in with Sandy's parole officer. I'm not mad at him as much as I'm tiring of his bull, and he knows it, too. Rah's been trying to talk to me since we arrived, but I've been busy with Mickey. Nellie's ignoring me and that's fine with me. She's a trip and a half, but as long as she's here for Mickey, I'm cool. Rah and I are waiting in the hallway outside of Mickey's room while Nigel and Mickey talk with the doctor about her labor's progression. Nellie and Chance made a coffee run. I guess she's talking to her gold toothed man again, but I'm not sure if Chance is feeling Nellie like he used to.

"So you are going to ignore me all night?" Rah asks, standing next to me. He smells good as usual, this time sporting Egyptian musk oil as his fragrance of choice, and it's working for him.

"Rah, I'm not ignoring you as much as I'm trying to keep my distance. Until you learn to respect my man, we can't chill like we used to." I look up at Rah and roll my eyes at his smiling ass. He's so full of himself it's ridiculous.

"Jayd, stop pushing me away. You know you want me right here," Rah says, breathing so close to me that we could share the same pulse. I swore I would never let him get this close to me again.

"No, Rah. I don't want you all up in my personal space. I share it with someone else now," I say, stepping away from him, but he doesn't let me go too far.

"Who, Jeremy?" Rah asks, flicking my gold bracelet hard with his right index finger, similar to the way Jeremy touched my ankh charm when he found out it was from Rah. I think they'd both rip them off and burn them if they could.

"Yes, Jeremy. He's my man now, not you."

"You should've asked me harder, Jayd, and we'd still be together." Is this fool serious?

"So let me get this straight. You wanted me to beg you to take me back, to keep you from sleeping with Sandy way back when, to not slang herb in the streets, therefore allow-ing your lunatic ex-girlfriend Trish to stay in your life until you change professions. Did I miss anything? All of the shit wrong in your life is my fault? Is that what you're saying to me, fool?" Whatever good these jade bracelets usually do for a sistah just went out the door with that ill logic.

"Well, when you say it like that it doesn't sound so good," Rah says, his chiseled ebony cheeks having lost some of their charm on me.

"You're damn right it doesn't sound good, because it's bull, Rah. None of that is my responsibility, especially not us breaking up. That was all your doing, every time you decided to cheat on me."

"All I'm saying is that if you had been a little sweeter to a nigga in the first place, none of this shit would be happening right now," Rah says. Now he's just getting indignant with his shit.

"I'm plenty sweet, and I'm not the one with the problem here. It's you."

"You could've asked me stronger. You could've insisted. You could've been a little sweeter to me, Jayd. Just admit it and I'll let it go," he says, lowering his voice. The nurses walking up the hall look at us curiously. We're the only other people in the hall talking, but there are plenty of couples on the floor having babies tonight.

"Like I said, I'm plenty sweet, Rah. I'm just not sweet enough for you." I turn around and knock on the door to Mickey's room, hoping they'll let me in. I have to get away from Rah and his warped logic.

"Come in," Mickey says. I open the door and see Mickey hooked up to the baby monitor, charting her labor's progress. The doctor's talking to the nurse and Mickey and Nigel are watching the monitor closely.

"How's it going?" I ask my friends, who look exhausted.

It's after ten and I know they're ready to go home, but their job is far from over, especially Mickey's.

"It's not," Mickey says, sounding pissed. "I've only dilated three centimeters in eight hours, Jayd. That ain't shit." The doctor looks at the nurse and then at us, exiting the room on that note.

"I'm sorry," I say, standing next to her bed where she and Nigel are laid out, comfortably spooning, which is what got them here in the first place. "Is there anything you need?"

"Yeah—for this baby to come out. Other than that, I'm good. My mom will be here when she gets off work later. My dad's pulling a double shift and can't make it until tomorrow afternoon." Mickey's parents are some of the hardest working people I know.

"You can tell everyone they can leave," Nigel says, yawning. "We'll call when something happens." Sounds good to me. I'm tired and need to get some sleep.

"Okay. I'll let everyone know and see you soon. Let me know if you need anything." I give them both a hug and head out of the room, turning the light off on the way out. Mickey needs to get as much rest as she can, and Nigel, too. I'm glad she's not in a lot of pain.

When I come back out into the hallway the entire gang is present.

"Y'all can go home. The labor is progressing slowly and there's nothing for us to do," I say, looking at the wall clock, ready to eat. We've been here all afternoon and evening and Mickey's only three centimeters in.

"But what if the baby comes and we're not here?" Nellie asks, speaking to me for the first time tonight. I can tell she's worried about our friend and that supersedes her jealousy for the time being.

"Then we'll meet her later," I say to Nellie. "Mickey's not in any pain yet, and she wants to rest. And believe me, she's going to need it to get through this." Mama's delivered her fair share of babies, and from what I've seen, labor can be very deceiving. Everything's calm now, but before we know it, it'll be time for Mickey to push, and all of this chilling she's doing now will be over. "Nigel and Mickey just want to relax right now." And so do I. My morning cramps have turned into my own personal cramps. I need to check myself before I leave. It's not a long drive from the West LA Kaiser Hospital to Inglewood, but it can be if I'm unknowingly bleeding all over the place.

"Let's bounce then, and give them their space," Rah says. Chance and Nellie are already at the elevator and Rah's waiting for me.

"I have to go to the bathroom. I'll be okay," I say, waving to them as the elevator arrives. I make my way to the women's restroom where my concern is validated. My period would have to start right now. I look inside my purse, praying my emergency pad is in the zipper pocket but it's not. Shit. Now what? I don't have any change for the ladies' supplies in the vending machine and don't want to walk back to the nurse's station like this.

I notice a woman's feet in the stall next to me. Hopefully she has an extra pad on her and I can get out of here.

"Excuse me," I say, tapping on the wall separating her stall from mine. "Do you have a pad?"

"Nope, but I've got tampons. Paper or plastic?" she asks. Damn. I hate using tampons, but beggars can't be choosers, especially not while squatting.

"Paper," I say, reaching under the wall and claiming the small monthly necessity. "Thank you."

"No problem. We've all been there." As she exits the stall to wash her hands, I rip the paper off and begin pushing. I can't wait to get home and get comfortable. My cramps are now full-blown and I'm in desperate need of my couch bed.

I'm miserable now, but it's nothing that some raspberry tea, a heating pad, and a good night's sleep can't cure. I have a long workday ahead of me tomorrow and so does Mickey if the baby doesn't get here soon.

I'm a soldier of love, Sade sings from my ringtone, waking me up. I have no idea what time it is. When I got home from the hospital last night, I fell into a deep sleep and have been there ever since. I worked all day and have a long day ahead of me at Mama's this afternoon. No matter how much work I have, it doesn't compare to what Mickey's going through. She's been in labor all weekend. They sent her home yesterday morning because her labor wasn't progressing. Mickey didn't want to take their drugs, under the advice of her mom who, after five children, knows what she's talking about. Mickey's been laboring at home ever since and is coping pretty well.

I called Jeremy to say goodnight before I passed out. He and his friends were hanging hard and probably still are, knowing them. I grab my phone and see Rah's name in the caller ID. I remember that Mickey's still in labor, even though it's technically Sunday morning. Maybe Rah's calling because she's finally ready to push that stubborn little girl out. Otherwise I wouldn't answer.

"Jayd, it's time," Rah says and I know what he's talking about, calling me at two in the morning. Why couldn't Nickey make her appearance at a decent hour and a day earlier? Already little mama's causing me to lose sleep, and I'm only her godmother, if Mickey hasn't changed her mind. If it were any other baby, I wouldn't care so much. But I already know Nickey Shantae is my spiritual godchild, and I have to be there for the birth and the rest of this child's life, starting today.

"Okay, I'm up," I say, kicking the blankets off and jumping

to my feet. I would've felt bad waking up Jeremy again if he were here.

"Do you want me to come get you? I'm already on my way to the hospital." Rah giving me a ride is dangerous, but so is me driving by myself this late with very little sleep and cramps. I have to take a Tylenol and keep pushing. I'd better pack one for the road and other supplies, too.

"Okay. I'll be ready when you get here," I say, flipping the phone shut and turning on the floor lamp next to the front door. I already have on sweats and a tank top. All I need is a sweater and some shoes and I'm ready to go. My gold silk scarf can stay on my fresh braids. There's no need to dress up for what I'm about to witness.

No, but you should at least wash your face and brush your teeth. You don't want to scare the poor child her first day out, my mom says in my head.

"Don't you ever sleep?" I ask aloud, as if she's standing right in front of me. I know she's right. As many times as me and my friends have awakened together after an all-night session, they won't be disturbed by my morning breath, but Nickey is new to the crew and deserves a sweet welcoming— fresh breath and all.

When Rah and I get back to Kaiser Hospital, Nellie and Chance are already there. Mickey's screaming can be heard all the way down the hall. I guess she's dilated more since we left a few hours ago.

"I'll let you handle that," Rah says, opening the door to Mickey's room for me. Mickey looks like hell. At least her mom's here to hold her hand and so is Nellie.

Mickey's near tears and ready to strip down to the bare necessities from the look of the sweat dripping down her face. "I want drugs. Lots of drugs!" she screams, but the nurse shakes her head.

"Oh, honey, it's too late for that. You've only got two more centimeters to go. You'll have to push the baby out the old-fashioned way," the same nurse from earlier says, checking Mickey out. "Don't worry, your body was designed for this." Mickey looks like she wants to kill the nurse and if she gets the chance to, she just might try. I step in between the two of them, ready to calm my girl down the best way I know how. But I have to get her to focus on me first and not the pain.

"Mickey, it's going to be okay," her mom says, feeding her daughter ice chips. Mickey's mom has been through this five times, and I know she's feeling for her eldest child. "Just breathe, baby."

"I don't want to do this anymore, Mama," Mickey says, looking more scared than I've ever seen my girl look before. Usually Mickey's fearless, but this shit has got her shook up, for real. "Tell them to make it stop, please," Mickey cries as another contraction hits. "Aaah!" Mickey's screaming is making me hurt, too. Nellie looks at our friend, terrified, and then up at me.

"I have to get some water," Nellie says, getting up from her chair and heading for the door. Something about the look on her face tells me our girl ain't coming back. Oh, no she doesn't. We all agreed to be here for Mickey and that's exactly what we're going to do.

I step outside the hospital room, catching Nellie before she can make her escape. "Where the hell are you going, Nellie? Mickey needs us to be here for her." I glance down the hall at the fathers' waiting room where our boys are chilling. It must be nice.

"We can't do anything for her," Nellie says, almost in tears. "She's got a baby coming out of her and from where I'm standing, there's not much I can do about it." Nellie looks nervously around the hospital hallway, rubbing her arms like she's cold. But with the long-sleeved American Eagle shirt and jeans she's wearing, I doubt she's chilly.

"What's wrong with you?" I ask. Nellie's acting like a drug addict in desperate need of a fix. "Why are you acting so strange, especially after the endless lectures on our duties as godparents? This shit is real, Nellie, and we need to be here for Mickey and the baby."

"I can't do it, okay!" Nellie shouts, shocking me and the three nurses working at their station. I'm sure this isn't the first time they've seen someone shouting in the hall, but usually that someone is pushing out a baby, not merely witnessing it. "This is way more than I bargained for. Mickey doesn't need me here for this."

"Oh, yes she does," I say, grabbing Nellie by her arms and shaking her. "This is exactly what you bargained for by being Mickey's friend. We don't get to choose when we're going to stick by her and when we're not, not if she's in need. And she needs us now more than ever, so suck it up and get back in that room." The nurses look like they want to cheer, but turn back to their work as Nellie glares their way.

"Jayd, I'm not as strong as you are. I can't take the pain." I look into Nellie's eyes, knowing she's talking about more than the labor.

"Nellie, you're not in any pain," I say, ready to shake the shit out of her once more. My cramps are starting to come back, so she'd better stop messing with me and get her narrow behind back in there. "Mickey's the one who's going through it."

"I know, but still. It's just too much to bear." I look into Nellie's eyes, ready to slap the shit out of her if need be, but I instead jump into her mind and cool her off, convincing her finally to go back into the room.

"Okay, you're right. Let's help our friend. After all, I was her back-up Lamaze partner and she kicked Nigel out, which means she'll need my help," Nellie says, reclaiming her crown as head godmother. As long as her ego's involved, Nellie will do what's called for.

"Exactly," I say, opening the door and escorting Nellie back inside. Mickey's still chomping on ice and panting like a thirsty dog. Her mother pats her glistening brow with a wet towel, but nothing's able to soothe our girl. "I guess it won't be too much longer," I say, noticing her contractions are coming faster according to the monitor. We were only outside for two minutes and already another one's coming.

"Ooooh," Mickey says, this time in a deeper pitch. "Aaah." It almost sounds like the type of moaning that got her into this mess, but from the looks of it, she's not enjoying this part at all.

"I'm out," Nellie says, raising her hands up and again leaving the room. Shit, now I have to focus on both of my friends' struggles. I look at Mickey and back at the closing door, ready to check Nellie's ass again.

"No, Jayd. Please don't leave," Mickey pleads, reaching out to me with her free hand. Her mom hasn't let go of her right hand since she got here. "I need you." I look at the door again and then at Mickey, deciding to help Mickey and leave Nellie to her own problems. Maybe it's good she's not here. I can only handle one drama queen at a time.

"I'm here, Mickey. And I'm not going anywhere." After all the drama me and this girl have been through, I still don't wish this pain on her. I look into Mickey's brown eyes, seeing the fear and uncertainty written all over her face, focusing intently on calming her mind down so she can get through the birth as peacefully as possible. I jump right in, noticing the baby is asleep. Good, because I can't handle little mama's sass right now. I have to get her mother through this before meeting her again.

Mickey's mind begins to cool at my entrance, but it's still

too hot for me to have an instant effect. Still moaning, Mickey grabs my hand and squeezes tightly, now allowing me full access to her experience. My friend's mind cools as I take all the heat.

"Ahhh," I say, feeling more than the pain Mickey's causing in my hand. I'm actually feeling her labor through my own cramps, each contraction more intense than the next. What the hell? I didn't sign up for this. I need to jump out of Mickey's mind and now. But I can't because Mickey—now completely relaxed—has closed her eyes, locking me in her mind's vision. Damn it. What the hell do I do now?

You grin and bear it, my mom says in my mind, while I'm in Mickey's. Now I know she knows my little secret.

Mom, how did you know? I think back, trying to focus on her thoughts and not the pain in my lower back and stomach. No wonder Mickey's so damn miserable. This shit really hurts. It feels like menstrual cramps magnified to the millionth degree. I'm surprised women still have babies if it feels like this.

I knew there was something strange going on when I entered your thoughts the other day and your mind felt unusually cool to me. I haven't felt that feeling in years, but you never forget, she says as another contraction hits, breaking my concentration. I can't groan as loud as I want because Mickey's mom will think something else is going on, but I can't hold it in too much longer, either. Mickey, on the other hand, is laid out like her unborn child. This is wrong on so many levels.

Okay, Mom. You got me. So how do I get out of this? I ask, wishing I'd never jumped in to begin with. This is Mickey's baby, not mine, so why I should I be the one to suffer?

You can't escape until Mickey regains consciousness and that might not be until the baby's being born. Next time be more careful when you jump in and know that you can get out, my mom says, jumping out of my mind. Damn it. I missed this chapter in the spirit book.

"Aaaah," I say. Mickey's mother looks at me like I'm tripping, and she's right. Mickey needs to wake up so I can get out of this mess and take a Tylenol. She can't take anything for her issues, but I sure as hell can try.

The sharp pain radiating down my back feels very much like when Esmeralda stabbed me in the dream I had a couple of weeks ago. Much like then, I'm blind to my surroundings and don't know which way is out. One major difference this time is that Mickey's baby will be born and this will be over. For my sake and Mickey's, I hope her daughter's birthday comes sooner than later, because I don't know how much more I can take. Mickey's been in labor for over thirty hours and we're still counting. I bet she's not going to rush into having a baby again after this experience.

"I have to push," Mickey says, diverting my attention from the pain coursing through my body. I can barely hear Mickey, I'm so out of it, but I can hear Mama speaking to me like she does in my dreams sometimes, telling me to snap out of it and remember to bring her back the afterbirth for a safe burial. I look at Mickey looking at me, freeing me from her mind.

"It's time," the nurse says, walking back into the room like she's the one having the baby. The doctor and another nurse also enter the room.

"You're doing great, Mickey," her mom says, holding her daughter's hand tightly. "She's almost here."

"Okay, on the next contraction push as hard as you can," the doctor says to Mickey from his front-row seat. Nigel walks in, ready to witness the birth of their daughter. I'm glad he's here and I think Mickey is, too. I let go of my girl's hand and reach for Nigel to take my place at her side. I've shared enough in the experience. It's time for the parents to do the pushing.

I've done all I can do as godmother and will make sure I take care of Nickey Shantae's spirit. After all, she is a caul girl like myself. I don't want her to end up having the same drama from the start because my mother let the hospital destroy my caul instead of paying it the proper reverence it's due. I'll make sure I get Nickey's caul after she makes her arrival, which should be any minute now. Mickey's pushing for her first Mother's Day, and we're all anxious to meet her little girl.

~ 10 ~
Mama's Day

*"Thank you Mama for the nine months you carried me through/
... No one knows the pressure you bear a just only you."*

—SIZZLA

At five-fifteen this morning, Mickey became the proud
mother of Nickey Shantae Esop. Both mother and child
are doing fine and resting well last time I checked. I've been
home for a couple of hours, unable to sleep because of this
morning's excitement. The birth was one thing, but convincing Mickey to ask for Nickey's caul from the nurses was another thing entirely. I had to tap into Mickey and the nurse's
minds at the same time. I didn't even know I could do that,
but with my mom's help we got it done—completely wiping
me out in the process. That coupled with me sharing
Mickey's labor has rocked me physically and mentally, yet I
still can't fall asleep.

My cell vibrates on the coffee table and I pick it up and answer without checking the caller ID. I'm too tired to care.

"Hello," I answer.

"Jayd, are you okay?" Mama asks, sounding concerned. It
must be after seven if Mama's already calling me.

"Yes, just tired. Mickey's baby was born early this morning," I say into the phone, realizing that won't excuse me
from today's festivities. Mama and Netta are very serious
about Mother's Day and it's an all-day affair for them. My
mom and Mama's other children all know the deal. I hope

Mama likes the stove we bought her. It should be delivered early this afternoon, and I want to make sure I'm there to receive it.

"Did you get the caul?" Mama asks. And people think I'm direct.

"Yes, ma'am," I say, yawning in the process. I really need to catch up on my sleep. "And I won't forget to bring it with me." I turn over on the couch, deeper into the pillows, trying to avoid the sun shining through the windows. We really need to get some darker shades.

"Good girl. I'll see you later, Jayd—but not too late. Catch a nap and come on. We need your help to feed the Mothers," Mama says, referring to our annual celebration of the eldest ancestors of them all. Most people fear the Mothers, calling them witches and all sorts of unholy names. But the truth is that if it weren't for them, nothing would exist. Our mother, Oshune, is over the Mothers and, as her daughters, we have a special relationship with them that is not to be ignored.

"I know, Mama. I'll see you in a little while." I hang up my cell, ready to pass out on the couch fully clothed, but not before Jeremy calls.

"Hello," I say groggily, but I'm glad to hear from my man.

"Hey, Jayd," Jeremy says. "How are Mickey and the baby doing?"

"They're fine. Tired, but fine," I say, smiling at the thought of Nickey and Mickey resting peacefully after a hard day's work on all of our parts—Nellie not included. That girl's a piece of work and then some. But I'll give her a piece of my mind later. Right now all I want to do is sleep.

"And how are you?" I love that I'm a priority in Jeremy's life, even if it is too early to call me this morning. Usually I'd be up for work and he'd be at the beach, unless he chose to sleep in.

"I'm good, Jeremy. But I do need to get some sleep before

going over to my grandmother's house today. We have a long afternoon planned and I haven't slept at all." I rub my lower back, remembering the labor pains I absorbed for Mickey. I hope she knows what a good friend she has in me. If not, I'll spend the rest of my life reminding her and so will Nickey. She remembers it, just like I remember bits and pieces of my birth. Having a vivid memory comes with being a caul child, as well as all the other gifts that can seem like a curse at times. Speaking of which, I'd better take some medicine before my cramps return and interrupt my eventual sleep.

"Okay, I won't hold you. I know you've had a long night and morning. Will you have some time to chill later?" I miss Jeremy, too, but it's going to be a full day and I need to visit Mickey at the hospital before visiting hours are over tonight.

"I honestly can't say, baby. It depends on how long we're at my grandmother's house and then after that I need to study," I say, remembering all the work I have ahead of me this last month of school. With cheer and the school play on my plate, I've got a lot going on. Not to mention the cotillion rehearsals, which begin as soon as school's out. At least my official presidential duties don't start until school starts again fall semester, allowing me somewhat of a break. I know summer's going to fly by, as usual, but I still welcome the warm break.

"I'll call you later to check on you. My mom's planned a brunch for the family and after that I'll be at the beach." Jeremy's so predictable. If he and Chance aren't working on their cars, they're at the beach surfing—not that Chance surfs much. But he does smoke and drink, also a favorite pastime of theirs.

"Have fun and tell your mother I said Happy Mother's Day." I don't really mean it, but I should be nice, even to my unofficial enemies.

"Same to your mom and grandmother, Jayd. I'll check you

later." I hang up the phone and settle under the covers, ready to fall into a deep sleep. Hopefully, I can get in a few good hours before getting up. I need to at least buy flowers and cards for all the mothers in my life. I tried to sneak in flowers with no greeting card last year, and Mama almost had a fit. She couldn't care less about me saving a few dollars. Mama wants the card, too, and I have to oblige. After all, it's her day, not mine.

After eating a quick breakfast, I quickly dress and head out the door. I got a good four hours of sleep and feel slightly rejuvenated. I can't wait to get a full night's rest tonight when I get back home, but that'll be hours from now. It's already after twelve and the day's just beginning. My mom sent me a text saying she'll meet me in Compton instead of here like we originally planned. I'm sure Karl did something special for her, even if I'm the one she should be spending Mother's Day with.

Last year, I made my mom breakfast and served her in bed, just like they do on the commercials. She loved it. This year we'll have to settle for a joint celebration, which is customary anyway. I just miss the one-on-one time my mom and I had before she met Karl. But it's all good. Maybe when they get married they can buy a house big enough for all of us to fit in, and then I can see my mom more often.

Before I leave, I need to call my stepmother, Faye, and make sure she got the card I sent her earlier this week. My brother and sister usually spend the day with their mom— my dad's first wife—so I know Faye feels alone because she has no children of her own. My dad didn't want any more kids and forbade Faye from getting pregnant, even though she is twenty years younger than him. That's messed up, to me, but it's their marriage and grown folks' business, as Daddy would say, which means I have no say in the matter.

"Happy Mother's Day," I say after Faye answers the phone. I'm glad she picked up and not my dad. He'll get his call next month on Father's Day, as always. Today is all about the women.

"Jayd, sweetie. How are you?" Faye asks. I can hear her smile through the phone. She's a sweet woman when she wants to be, but she has her moments.

"I'm good. Did you get the card I sent?" I ask while I check my outfit in the mirror one more time. I opted for some simple purple yoga pants and a gray top. We have a lot of spirit work to do, and I know I'll be required to change into my whites at some point, so there's no point in getting all dressed up.

"Yes, I did. Thank you very much. Your father told me you went to the eye doctor. How'd that go?" she asks, checking on her investment. Technically we're all on her insurance, and because she works for a state school, she gets the best benefits.

"I haven't gone yet," I say. I refuse to drive nearly thirty miles to see the eye doctor or the dentist.

"Jayd, you really should take advantage of having good insurance available to you. Everyone doesn't."

"You're right, and I've been meaning to ask if it's all right to change my dentist and optometrist to a closer location. I called customer service and they said I only need your social security number and they'll approve the transfer." Faye pauses slightly and I already know the answer's no, but it was worth a shot. For some reason, she doesn't trust me unconditionally like my mother does. I know all my mom's and Mama's information, just in case I ever need it one day.

"Oh, Jayd. I'm not comfortable with that," Faye says as if I asked her for a loan. "Besides, the whole family goes to Long Beach. That's the way it's always been. You're driving your mother's car, right?" she asks, sounding just like her hus-

band. Why did I even bother? Talking to one is just like talking to the other.

"Yeah. I have to go," I say, ready to end this conversation.
One minute more is too long for me. "Happy Mother's Day,
Faye. I hope you have a great one."

"To your mom, too, Jayd." Ending the call, I rush out of
the house, lock the door, and jog down the stairs. I don't
want to miss Mama's gift being delivered or the look on her
face when she sees it. I'll stop at Ralphs and grab the flowers
and cards before hopping on the freeway. I should also pick
up something for Mickey since it's her first Mother's Day,
too. How cute is it that Nickey showed up today, out of all
the days she could've been born? That girl knows she's
special.

When I arrive on Gunlock Avenue, practically the entire
block is hanging out on this beautiful Sunday afternoon. I
love May weather. I can smell Mama and Netta's cooking all
the way down the block, or perhaps my nose is extra sensitive to the way they get down. I take the flowers and cards
out of the passenger's seat and exit the car, ready for our celebration.

"Where's Lynn Marie, Jayd? I thought she was coming with
you." Mama asks, eyeing her candy, cards, and other gifts.
There's so much stuff we can hardly see the dining room
table. Her godchildren spoil her on this day especially, and
her sons look like they chipped in, too. There are even more
gifts on the coffee table. After what I witnessed this morning,
mothers deserve all this and more for what they go through
bringing life into the world. The job is no joke.

"She's on her way," I say, placing the gifts I brought and
the bag containing Nickey's caul on one of the four dining
room chairs with my purse. Netta's singing in the back, hard
at work.

"Your mama being on time for once would be a good gift," Mama says, spotting a box of See's candy, our favorite. Maybe she'll share some of that with me later. Aside from Netta's melodic voice, I can hear something large coming down the narrow street. I peek out the window to see a huge appliance truck and the drivers are looking for what I assume is Mama's address. It's here and just in time, too. I'm sorry my mom's not here yet, but we can't wait on her forever.

"Your real gift's outside," I say, pointing to the delivery-man exiting the large vehicle. His partner hops out on the passenger's side, all set to help with the delivery.

"What did you do?" Mama says, opening the screen door and stepping onto the front porch with Lexi and me right behind her.

"We bought you what you needed and wanted this year—a new stove." I step off the porch, sign the delivery papers and watch as they unload the appliance off the truck.

"You want this to go through the front or back, miss?" one of the drivers asks. Netta walks up the driveway from the back yard, smiling.

"Yes, the back is fine," I yell. My uncles come out of the garage where they're all hanging out, smoking and watching television, to see what's going on. Even Daddy, home early from church for a change, looks on, curious, at the oversized box being wheeled into the backyard. Jay, already in the kitchen, looks out the window, watching them maneuver the gift indoors.

"We'll have the old one moved out and this one hooked up in no time, Ms. Jackson," the deliveryman says, mistaking me for my mother, who shares my last name even if she's been divorced for almost as long as I've been alive—but not for much longer. After she and Karl tie the knot, I'll be the only Jackson around here.

"Jayd, where did you get the money for this?" Mama exclaims, completely surprised by the delivery. She watches the men unplug the old stove. If I didn't know better, I'd say this old thing actually appears relieved to finally be laid to rest.

"I've been saving my money, just like you taught me to," I say, smiling at Mama's joy. It's about time she had something she wanted.

"I've been praying for a new stove for so long, baby. Thank you," Mama says, hugging me tightly with tears in her eyes. Daddy and the boys look completely foolish as we embrace. How could Daddy not know Mama wanted this, when she's been hinting about it forever? I wish it would fit in the back-house and we could move that stove in here, since this is where everyone else also cooks. I really don't want the men touching the stove.

"Hey, Jayd, if you ballin' like that you should let a nigga hold something," my uncle Kurtis says, almost ruining the mood. But I choose to ignore his ignorant ass and focus on Mama's smile. My other three uncles eye the stove carefully, touching the clean, white knobs as the deliverymen finish hooking it up before taking the old one away.

"Don't touch it," Mama says, stepping in front of her gift like she'll be able to protect it from getting used. Good luck with that. With the exception of Daddy, Bryan, and Jay, these fools around here have no respect for people or their things. If they did, they wouldn't be living with their parents well into their thirties.

"Yeah, I'm with Mama," I say, stepping to the side of the new acquisition and protecting it fully. "Y'all can use the microwave from now on. This is for Mama's use only."

"Whatever, Jayd," Jay says, laughing at our vehemence, but Mama and I are serious. We know they'll eventually mess it up and that's not okay with me. One of these punks always ruins a good thing, and I'm determined not to let that happen this time around, especially not to Mama. She's been through enough and her tired eyes say she's still going through it.

"What's going on here?" my mom asks, walking into the dining room through the front door. "Oh, it came already? I wanted to be here for the delivery," she says, closing the front door behind her. As usual, my mom looks stunning in a cream, off-the-shoulder jumpsuit with pumps to match. Her long ebony hair is flat-ironed and hanging down her back, her green eyes sparkling. The beauty of their older sister takes even my uncles aback. Let the hating officially begin.

"Look what the cat dragged in," my uncle Junior says before retreating down into the den off the living room, which he and two of his brothers share. How Bryan, Jay, and Daddy ended up sharing the bedroom next to Mama's bedroom I don't know. But it just worked out like that.

"Well, hello to you, too," my mom says after her brother. "Hey, y'all. Happy Mother's Day, Mama," she says, walking over to Mama and hugging her tightly with flowers in her hand.

"You knew about this, Lynn Marie?" Mama asks, overwhelmed all over again by the surprise. Not much gets past Mama, but we got her good this time.

"Of course I knew about it. Who do you think helped pay for this thing?" My mom checks out her investment, winking at me in the process. "You did good, Jayd. I couldn't have picked out a better stove myself." My mom can be cute when she wants to. She was up in my head the whole time I shopped for the damn thing, telling me what to look for and how much was too much, since she maxed out most of her credit cards. I gave her my half in cash and she charged the purchase so we could get it delivered on time. Having them hook it up and remove the old stove was a whole other issue, and expensive, but well worth every dime.

"My girls," Mama says, taking both my mom and me in her

arms, allowing her emotions to flow. Netta comes in from outside and joins in the hugging. My mom and I join in the tear fest, making the men in the room uncomfortable. My uncle Kurtis joins his brother in the den, bored with the love in the room.

"Well, let's see what this baby can do," my uncle Bryan says, slapping his hands together and licking his lips like he's about to get something good to eat. But unless he's going to Wendy's or somewhere, he's in for a rude surprise.

"I'm serious, boy. There will be no cooking on my stove," Mama says, releasing us from our group hug and smacking Bryan's hand. She emphasized the word *my* like it's a baby she just gave birth to. He'd better back up if he knows what's good for him.

"Lynn Mae, you can't be serious," Daddy says, laughing at his wife, but she's not joking. He then looks at the dozen roses and card he bought Mama, sitting on the dining room table with all the other flowers and cards, suddenly feeling inadequate. It's not my fault he didn't hear Mama every time she asked for the same thing repeatedly. I don't know why Daddy didn't buy what Mama said she wanted. But maybe he'll listen more closely the next time Mama asks.

"The hell I'm not," Mama says, staring at the stove. "I better not catch anyone using my stove, you hear? Or I'll never cook for any of you again—ever." All the men laugh at first, knowing Mama makes that threat a few times every day. But it's apparent that Mama's very serious this time.

"All right, girls. Let's get to the spirit room. We have a lot of work to do," Netta says, heading back outdoors. "The Mothers aren't going to feed themselves." Netta's more excited about the festivities than Mama, who eyes her gift one last time before exiting the kitchen. I quickly grab my purse and Nickey's bag, following Mama out with my mom right behind us.

Most of the work we have to do is outside by the old fig tree. Mama consecrated that tree when she moved here over thirty years ago. Unfortunately, it sits in the corner of the yard that separates our house from Esmeralda's. I'm grateful for the back gate, even though it's in desperate need of repair. The bushes maintain some of our privacy, but Esmeralda can see everything from her back porch. I notice Misty and her mom also celebrating the day with their evil godmother. Lucky us.

"This is where we'll bury the baby's caul," Mama says. "We'll also pray to the Mothers before finishing dinner." My mom and I look at each other, acknowledging that we have a long afternoon ahead of us. My stomach begins to growl, signaling I should have eaten more than the bowl of cornflakes I had for breakfast.

Netta's already set up for the rituals. There's a white sheet spread out on the ground in front of the tree with several bowls of water, various herbs, and pictures of birds, the animal manifestation of the Mothers. Netta and Mama remove their shoes and step onto the sheet, each picking up a bowl of water. My mom and I remain on the grass, allowing Mama and Netta to do their thing.

"Our Mothers are often mistaken for being mean, taking life when necessary and wreaking havoc when the world is unbalanced. But the truth is, they are the balance," Mama says, pouring the libation and officially beginning the ceremony of reverence.

"Oshune is over cool waters. Her children have a natural inclination to want to keep a cool head, even when things are very hot around them. This is also part of the balance," Netta says, pouring the holy water on the ground. She then passes me the shovel to begin digging a spot for the caul. My mom picks up one of the other bowls and pours the water in the same spot, softening the earth, making it easier to dig.

"We, the Mothers' daughters, honor you on your day," Mama says, she and Netta pouring the remaining water onto the base of the tree. She then claims the bag, praying over the baby's birth membrane. I keep digging, also praying for my goddaughter and her mother. I pray that Mickey's a good mother, unlike Sandy, and that she always puts Nickey first in her life. I also pray I'm the best friend and godmother I can be. I'll do anything for that little girl—spiritual or otherwise. We're getting her off to a great start by providing her with spiritual protection. It's up to her parents to give her the rest of the nourishment she needs, and I'll be there to fill in the gaps when they don't.

We had a beautiful afternoon, praying and singing outside. Each of us feels good about the work we're doing, and can't wait to reap the benefits. Mama and Netta have been cooking all day and the food's almost done.

"It's all about the balance," Mama says, first pouring apple cider vinegar and then brown sugar into the greens, making my stomach growl. I'm so glad the Mothers like soul food. We get to enjoy the benefits of feeding them, too. "I say we bake the cornbread in my new oven, since this one is full," Mama says, leading us out of the spirit room and toward the main house. "This way, ladies."

We walk out of the stuffy house, grateful for the evening breeze.

"Is something burning?" my mom asks, smelling the same thing we all do in the warm air, and it's coming from Mama's kitchen.

Unable to run with the heavy skillet in her hands, Mama walks fast toward the back door.

"Who the hell already broke my damn stove?" Mama yells at the top of her lungs, which is very loud. Everyone stops and stares, afraid to breathe should she think it's an admission of guilt. I know Mama knows it wasn't me, but I'm still not stupid enough to let a peep out, either.

"Lynn Mae, let me take this out of your hands," Netta says, stepping beside Mama and removing the unbaked bread from her friend's trembling hands. She sets it down on the kitchen table and puts her left arm around Mama's shoulders. Mama's crying, she's so mad. Like Mama said, you should never upset the Mothers and this one is very pissed off.

"Lynn Mae, what's all this fussing about?" Daddy asks, apparently unaware of the verbal memo circulating through the thick air. "I heard you yelling all the way down the street."

"The brand new stove Jayd and little Lynn bought me for Mother's Day is burnt the hell up, that's what I'm fussing about, you jackass," Mama says to Daddy, who is now sorry he said a word. When Mama's pissed, innocence is irrelevant and punishment swift. Daddy looks around the living room at his four sons, daughter, grandson, and granddaughter, all of us afraid to make the next move. Netta holds on to Mama tightly, lending her a calmness that only a true homegirl can bring.

"I'm a grown-ass man," my uncle Kurtis says. "It was me." Stupid is as stupid does, and saying that shit was his first mistake. "I forgot I was warming up some chili fries, and fell asleep." My uncle Kurtis turns around and walks toward the den, apparently thinking he's going to be able to walk away from Mama unscathed. Like Daddy and my uncle Bryan and cousin Jay, I move out of the line of fire because I know something's about to fly through the air and hit my uncle Kurtis square in the head. Junior should consider moving in case of a ricochet effect, but he holds tight, posted up by the couch.

"I can't keep nothing in this house—not a damn thing!"

Mama yells, taking off her sandal and throwing it at Kurtis like it's a hand grenade. Knowing the soft shoe didn't hurt, Mama claims a hard wooden brush from the coffee table and throws it at him, this time making an impact on his otherwise hard head.

"Damn, that shit hurt, man," Kurtis says, rubbing the back of his head. He continues to take the single step down into the den and Mama's on him like a lion on a giraffe: The latter may be visibly larger, but everyone knows the lion will be the victor in the end.

"That's it! I've had it," Mama says, hitting my uncle like he stole something. Daddy goes after Mama, pulling her off their son.

"She's crazy, man," my uncle says, rubbing his sore head. Mama frees herself from Daddy and heads toward the kitchen. She opens the broom closet, which is anything but clean, and claims the old wood-and-straw tool like it's a weapon.

"I've been too damn nice about y'all trifling, grown-ass men living up in my house. I want you out in seven days, do you hear me? Out, out, out!" Mama wipes the sweat from her brow with the back of her hand and charges back outside, slamming the door shut behind her. This is the rawest I've ever seen her, and I've seen Mama get real hot in my day. I wonder if she'll really follow through with evicting her precious boys. With one of her sons dead and the other one willfully missing in action, these are her last four at home. She has a hard time letting go of her children and grandchildren, no matter how old they are.

"Daddy, she's talking crazy, right?" my uncle Kurtis asks, but even he knows once Mama has spoken, it's a wrap. The broom says it all.

In the spirit book it says that if someone sweeps a broom in your direction, you're cursed. There are also many other stories about ways to use brooms for protection and to make someone sick. Kurtis has to be out in seven days or Mama will have his ass in a sling—literally. It's a shame we went from enjoying a lovely afternoon to this mess. And because of my trifling uncle, I'm sure the evening is over, and on a sour note at that. I guess I'll take my dinner to go. I need to visit Mickey before it's too late, but I didn't want Mama's day to end like this. If I could kick Kurtis's ass myself, I would. But I'll have to trust in Mama's work to do the trick—it always does.

Epilogue

Netta took Mama out for the rest of the evening and that's just what she needs: a break from the norm. Luckily the stove is under warranty. I'm not sure if it'll cover dumb-ass fools leaving the oven on, but we'll see. My mom promised to handle it and I'm grateful she's taken the responsibility off my shoulders. I have enough to do and I need to get some good sleep tonight after I come home from the hospital. Jeremy's meeting me at the apartment later. I'm sure he needs to wind down, too.

The traffic is light from Compton to West Los Angeles this evening. Mickey's flowers are slightly wilted from the long day, but will hopefully make her smile anyway. While stopped at a red light, my phone rings and I answer Rah's call.

"Hey, girl," Rah says, sounding as tired as we all are. "If you haven't gone to the hospital yet, can you pick me up? I let Nigel take my car this morning because he left his car at the hospital when his father picked him up." Why am I always Rah's go-to person?

"Rah, I told you I'm not falling for your bull anymore," I say, watching the traffic turn in front of me. My light should be turning green soon. I have to hang up or risk getting a ticket for talking on my cell while driving.

"Jayd, this is the last time I'll ask you for anything, other than braiding my hair, I promise," Rah says, making me smile. "I'm going to respect your space from now on, girl. You can trust me." Rah may be telling the truth, but I'm a long way from trusting the brotha. I'll give him a ride only because Nigel's my friend and Rah is Nickey's godfather. We're in this together, whether I like it or not.

"I'll see you in ten minutes, Rah," I say, making a left on La Cienega Boulevard. He's lucky I have to pass by his house to get to the hospital anyway.

When I pull up in Rah's driveway, Sandy's showing her ass, as usual. I guess Rah confronted Sandy about the visit from her parole officer and their fake engagement. It doesn't look like she's taking it so well. If I have to see Rah on a regular basis, this girl's got to go. I hope he's kicking her ass out once and for all, Mother's Day be damned.

"But where am I supposed to go?" Sandy screams after Rah, who greets me before passing me up on his way to his bedroom as I enter the front door. He gave his room to Sandy and Rahima and sleeps in his studio. "You know you can't be without your little girl."

"She's not a carrot, Sandy. And you'd better enjoy her while you can, because the first chance I get I'm taking my daughter away from you," Rah yells from his room. Frantically dialing his cell, he starts throwing Sandy's shit in the middle of the hallway on the floor. This is getting too ugly for me.

"You'll never have Rahima without me—never." She walks to the back with a now frantic Rahima on her hip, screaming at the top of her lungs. Luckily Rah's little brother, Kamal, is at their grandparents' house and shielded from this bull. I wish I could say the same for their daughter.

"Rah, I have to go," I say from the foyer. "I want to see the baby before visiting hours are over." And I don't want to wit-

ness what I'm sure is going to be a beat-down on somebody's watch. Every time I come over here, there's drama. I
can't wait until Sandy's finally out of our lives for good.

"Wait up, Jayd. I'm coming with you," Rah says, throwing
the last of Sandy's things out of his reclaimed room and locking the door behind him. "And so is Rahima."

"The hell she is," Sandy says, sorting through her strewn
clothes like she's shopping at Goodwill for strippers. "You're
not taking my daughter anywhere, especially not with that
witch." There's that word again, and on Mother's Day, too.
Now the shit's personal. I've been too nice for too long with
this heffa.

"You shouldn't throw around words like that haphazardly,
Sandy. They may get you into more trouble than you bargained for." Sandy straightens her five-eleven frame, finally
letting Rahima off her hip. As her daughter runs toward her
daddy, Sandy charges at me and I'm ready for the impact.

"You crazy bitch! I could mop the floor with your midget
ass," Sandy says, going for my hair, like most girls do in the
heat of battle. She's lucky this isn't a Pam Grier movie. Otherwise Sandy's fingers would be bleeding profusely by now for
snatching on my fresh do. But I've got something better for
her ass—and a lot colder.

Sandy pulls my head back, forcing me to look at her wild
ass. I stare at her hard and call off Rah with my right hand—
he's about to snatch her up like the poisonous weed she is.
Looking into Sandy's enraged eyes, I go full throttle on this
broad's mind. I owe it to my first goddaughter to rid her of
her unhealthy mother until Sandy gets her act together.
That's the best Mother's Day present for us all.

"You will leave Rahima with her daddy and go get yourself
some help. Now, Sandy," I say. I hope her hot head responds
to my persuasion quickly, because I don't know how much
longer I can let her hold me like this without pimp-slapping

her ass good, just out of reflex. Rah and Rahima stare at us, frozen in the moment like we all are. I can see Sandy's mind altering, bending to my rational thoughts as I repeat my wishes in her mind. She's a hot mess—literally. I feel sorry for her, but she needs to get the hell away from their daughter before it's too late. I already know what kind of havoc Sandy can wreak, and refuse to allow Rahima to be a victim of her mother's irrational behavior any longer. Much like Misty, Sandy doesn't know which way to go on her own.

Sandy releases her hold on my hair, still looking at me and I at her. She stands erect, now sure of what she needs to do, but I'm not letting go of her until she's actually out.

"I'm tired of this shit," Sandy says, shaking her head and looking around, dazed and confused. One thing is perfectly clear: Her time living at Rah's has run out. "I'm going to stay with my grandparents."

"Not with Rahima," Rah says, picking up his daughter, who looks frightened by the scene. I'm sorry for my role in that, but I had no choice. "She's staying here with me." Rah looks from Sandy to me, noticing something else is going on, but he's not sure what. It's none of Rah's business because I'm not doing this for him, Sandy, or myself. This is all about baby girl. I have a feeling I'll be doing this a lot for Nickey's parents, too. I might as well get my practice in now. Continuing the mental ass-kicking, I wait until Sandy's head is completely cool before easing up off of her.

"Fine, keep her," Sandy says, letting go of me. "I'm tired of worrying about babysitting, food, diapers and shit anyway." That's just what I wanted to hear. I let her eyes and mind go, allowing her to pick up her clothes from the hallway floor and pack the rest of her shit. I'll drive her ass to Pomona myself if I have to, as long as she doesn't come back to LA anytime soon. With her gone and Rahima in Rah's possession, he should be one step closer to gaining permanent custody of his daughter. I don't know if Sandy can keep her job, but I'm sure they have strip clubs by her grandparents' house, too. Rah looks stunned by Sandy's seemingly easy change of heart, but doesn't contest.

"Jayd, let's go," Rah says, taking his daughter and leading the way out of the wrecked house. Rah certainly has his work cut out for him when he gets home. Between all of the mental work I did at the hospital last night and tapping into Sandy's mind, I'm feeling a little light-headed. Maybe a good night's rest will take care of it. I have too much to do to risk having a meltdown now.

Drama High, Volume 12:

PUSHIN'

L. Divine

ABOUT THIS GUIDE

The following questions are intended to
enhance your group's reading of
DRAMA HIGH: PUSHIN'
by L. Divine.

DISCUSSION QUESTIONS

1. Mickey and Nigel have decided to be a couple despite the inevitable challenges that come with being teenage parents. Do you think it's a good idea, especially now that we know that Nigel is not the father of Mickey's baby?
2. Now that Chance knows his true lineage, is he responding the right way? Should he change his name to his birth name, Chase, or stick to Chance?
3. Is Jayd taking on more than she can handle with her new responsibilities coupled with her spirit work, her job, and her side hustle? If she has to choose between them, which ones should she keep and which should she let go?
4. Is Jeremy right to be jealous of Jayd's friendships with Rah and Mr. Adewale?
5. Have you ever considered becoming a debutante? Why or why not? Do you think it's a good idea for Jayd to be involved?
6. Is Mrs. Esop a good role model for Jayd? Do you think Jayd should become more active in the sorority that is sponsoring her?

7. If you could absorb your friend's pain, would you?

8. If you could choose one of the Williams women's gifts of sight, which would you choose, and why? What would you do with your powers?

9. Do you have any meddlesome and antagonistic neighbors like Esmeralda? Do you sympathize with them or do you want them to move out?

10. Is Rah right to kick Sandy out? Should he give her one more chance or let her go for good? Why or why not?

Jaydism #4

When it's that time of the month, try natural remedies to ease your discomfort. For example, drinking raspberry tea eases cramps, and chamomile tea relaxes you. Essential oils, herbal teas, and elevating your legs while lying down are time-proven solutions. A heating pad and sprinkling lavender oil around the room works wonders, too. Get plenty of rest and relax. As my grandmother would say to me, "This too shall pass," and it always does.

Stay tuned for the next book in
the DRAMA HIGH series,
THE MELTDOWN

Until then, satisfy your DRAMA HIGH craving
with the following excerpt from the next
exciting installment.

ENJOY!

Jayd's Journal

My mom always keeps an ink pen and pad in her glove compartment in case she needs to write something down while in the car. Now that I'm the main driver for her aging Mazda Protegé, I use the tools to write about anything significant that may have happened in my day before I forget, no matter where I am, which in this case is in the parking lot of Ralphs grocery store in the Ladera Center. We're not too far from Rah's house, also the scene of my latest chick fight with Rah's ex-girlfriend, Sandy. I can't believe she let me inside of her mind—after she manhandled me—and that I got her to give up their daughter, Rahima, and finally move out of Rah's house. He owes me big-time for handling his baby-mama drama for him.

I've been using my mom's powers like crazy, learning how to master them but still not able to control my dreams, which is where my true power lies. It's crazy, I know, but not crazier than Mama going off on her sons earlier this afternoon. Now that was some serious drama, and on Mother's Day, too. She and Netta left to cool Mama's head. It's bad enough she has to live with my trifling uncles every day of the week, but the one day of the year they should be grateful to her, one of them screwed it up by burning up the new stove my mom and I bought her. Mama made it perfectly clear that she's had it, and I'm with her.

Rah had to run inside the market for diapers on our way to pick up Nigel, and he took Rahima with him. Mickey's waiting for us, at the hospital, even if we can't stay long because it's getting late. Nigel's going to spend the night at the hospital with Mickey and her new baby, and his dad will pick him up in the morning. And since Rah's car is already there, I really just have to drop him and his daughter off, say hi to Mickey and my goddaughter, and call it a night. This has been one of the longest days of my life, and as such calls for a good night's sleep. Even with school in the morning, it's the last month before summer and I couldn't be happier. We all need a break from the madness that is Drama High.

Prologue

When Rah, Rahima, and I arrive at Nigel's house, Mrs. Esop is enjoying the sunset from her garden view on the front porch. Great. Another tough broad to deal with, but I actually respect this one, even if I don't feel like socializing today. I just want to bless my godchild one more time and go home.

"Jayd, it's lovely to see you, my dear," Mrs. Esop says, rising from the patio chair to give me a hug. "And look at this little princess. Rahima looks more and more like you every day, Raheem." And she's right. Rah couldn't deny his namesake if he tried, not that he ever would. After all the hell he's been through, first trying to find his daughter the first time Sandy ran off, and then once again after he did find her. Rah loves his daughter with all he's got and then some.

Mrs. Esop squeezes Rahima's cheeks gently, making the little girl smile and hide behind her daddy. She can play that shy role all she wants, but I know Rahima's a natural born ham and deserves all the attention she can get.

"Thank you, and happy Mother's Day," Rah says, handing Mrs. Esop a box of Godiva chocolates he just purchased on our pit-stop, and from the look on her face, she's very pleased. What girl doesn't love chocolates?

"Oh, baby, you didn't have to do that, but I'm so glad you did," Mrs. Esop says, taking the gold box and hugging her play-son. Since Rah's mom isn't around—even on her own holiday—Mrs. Esop's always there for him. "Rah, there are some fresh cookies on the counter. Why don't you give Rahima one while you wake up my son, who's asleep on the living room couch? Jayd, how are you enjoying this lovely Sunday?" she says, expertly excusing Rah from our conversation. I'm too tired for this, but it doesn't look like I have much of a say in the matter.

"I'll be back in a minute, Jayd," Rah says, taking the not-so-subtle hint and heading through the front door hand in hand with his toddler.

"Jayd, aren't you glad that wasn't you in labor this morning?" Mrs. Esop asks, sipping her tea and gesturing for me to join her in the chair across from hers. It must be nice to pass the time in luxury. If she only knew I actually did share the labor with Mickey, she'd eat her words.

"Yes, ma'am. But Mickey handled it like a pro." Why I just lied, I don't know. But I feel obligated to stand up for my girl because I know where this conversation is going.

"You look a little troubled, Jayd. Everything okay?" I checked myself in the visor mirror when I got in the car, but haven't had a chance to fully recoup from my run-in at Rah's. I hate it when a trick pulls my hair. It messes up the entire flow of my ponytail.

"Sandy moved back to her grandparents' house. I helped her pack," I say, still unable to process the thought. Is Sandy really gone for good? I know Mrs. Esop knows I'm lying about helping Sandy. Everyone knows we aren't friends, but I'm not going to tell Mrs. Esop I was in another fight. She thinks I'm growing into a nice young lady and I'm trying. But bitches are everywhere and sometimes they have to be dealt with properly.

"Ah," Mrs. Esop says, taking one of the freshly cut pink roses from the clear vase on the table, bringing it to her nose and inhaling deeply. "Girls like Sandy are never gone for good, Jayd. Mark my words—that girl will be back." Mrs. Esop looks at me, her brown eyes narrowing at the truth in her words. I know she's not fully aware of my powers, but she knows Mama and our lineage so I know she knows more than she's not saying.

"Nigel will be out in a second," Rah says, stepping back onto the front porch with Rahima, who's happily munching on the baked treat. "Jayd, you ready to roll?"

"Yes, it is getting late and I know Mickey's wondering where we are," I say as I rise from my seat. I lean back and steady myself on the glass table before nearly falling back into my chair, suddenly feeling light-headed. What the hell?

"Jayd, are you okay?" Rah asks, letting go of his daughter's hand and grabbing me by the arm, helping me catch my balance. Mrs. Esop rises and takes my other arm with a concerned look on her face.

"Sit down," Mrs. Esop says, directing me to reclaim my seat, but I can't. The pounding in my head creeps from the back of my skull all the way to the front, dulling all other sounds around me. It feels like a brain freeze but much more painful. I look up at Mrs. Esop, who now appears to be Maman, my great-grandmother. I try to scream at the sudden visual transformation, with no success. Before I can let out a sound, Maman's gone and so is the pounding, but I still feel woozy. Between my lack of sleep, inadvertently sharing Mickey's labor, and dealing with Sandy's crazy ass I'm completely wiped out.

"What's going on?" Nigel says, stepping out of the open front door looking as exhausted as I feel.

"Jayd's not feeling well. Nigel, get her some water," Mrs. Esops says, now forcing me to sit down, and I allow her to push me back into the chair. Maybe I do need to chill for a spell. Nigel walks back into the house and Rahima follows, undoubtedly going back for another cookie, completely oblivious to my issues. If life were only that simple for us all.

"I'm fine, really. I probably just need some rest." What was that? I've never seen Maman so clearly outside of my dreams before. It was as if she took over Mrs. Esop's body for a moment, but I know that can't be.

"There's no probably about it, girl," Rah says, feeling my forehead like Mama does when she hears me make the slightest sniffle. "You need to chill."

"Maybe we should drop you off at home, Jayd. Mickey will understand," Nigel says, placing a cool glass of water down on the table in front of me. I pick up the crystal cup with both hands and bring it to my lips, sipping slowly at first and then swallowing the rest in two large gulps.

"Thirsty, baby?" Rah asks, smiling down at me, but it's no joke. I feel like I ate a block of salt for dinner and Mama doesn't cook with that much sodium.

"Yes, I am." I hand Rah the glass and he hands it to Nigel. "Can I have some more water, please?" They all look at me, amazed. It was a tall glass, but damn. Can't a sistah get something to quench her thirst?

"Okay, now I know something's wrong. I'm taking you home, now." Rah uses both hands to check my temperature, now annoying me. I gently swat his hands away from my face and attempt again to rise from the chair. Mrs. Esop looks at me and then at Rah and I know what she's thinking—literally.

"Mrs. Esop, I can assure you I'm not pregnant with Rah's baby or anyone else's for that matter," I say, steadying myself before letting go of the glass table. "I'm a virgin and plan on staying that way for a long time."

"Jayd, how did you know that's what I was thinking?" Mrs. Esop's look of concern has turned into one of fear. She obviously knows I repeated her thoughts verbatim—all without focusing on cooling her mind and allowing me in, like I usually do with my mom's powers. It was as if she threw the thought my way and I unintentionally caught it. I have to get my mom's powers on lock and fast, before they get ahead of me.

"It was written all over your face," I say, taking the cool drink from Nigel's hands, swallowing it down quickly and returning the empty glass to him. "We should get going if we're going to make it before visiting hours are over. We only have an hour left," I say, glancing at Rah's wristwatch.

"The only place you're going is home," Rah says, helping me off the porch and down the driveway where we're parked. "Don't worry about the car situation. We'll work it out."

"Yeah, man. Drive her home. Mom, can I take your car?" Nigel asks. I know his mom wants to say no, but under the circumstances she reluctantly nods her head affirmatively. I wouldn't want to give up the Jaguar either.

"You guys don't have to do that. I can make it home," I say and I can. "Thank you for the hospitality, Mrs. Esop, and I'll see you next weekend for the debutante meeting. The water was just what I needed to feel better." Nigel and Rah look at each other and reluctantly follow me to my car, retrieving Rahima's car seat and letting me go.

"Feel better, Jayd," Mrs. Esop says, staring at me strangely. I know she's tripping about sharing her thoughts with me, but what can I say? I didn't do it on purpose and I doubt I can do it again—at least not willingly. I have a lot to learn about my mom's gift of sight, and will read up on it more but not tonight. I just want to wash Sandy's fingerprint out of my hair, watch my Sunday night television shows and pass out on my mom's couch—no scary visions or crazy broads permitted.

"The men all pause."

—Klymaxx

Rah and Nigel must've texted and called me fifty times on the way from Nigel's hood in Lafayette Square to my mom's apartment in Inglewood. It's not a long drive because both areas are off of Crenshaw Boulevard and it doesn't require much thought to get here. I understand their concern and sent them a message as soon as I pulled in a few minutes ago. I'm glad to have my mom's space to park in so I don't have to worry about walking down the block by myself late at night. Making it to the front door and up the stairs from the sunken carport is challenging enough.

"Hey, girl," my mom says, surprising me as I open the multi-locked front door. What's she doing here so late? Usually she'd be with her man, Karl, especially after spending the day with us at Mama's house. Maybe he had dinner plans with his mom for the special day.

"Hey, Mom," I say, closing the door behind me. From the looks of it, my mom came home to restock her clothes. She took the jar of quarters from her dresser and put them in one of the three laundry baskets on the living room floor. I guess she's finally run out of clean clothes. Although knowing my mom, she probably ran out weeks ago and just bought new ones to wear for the time being, which I'm sure got a little expensive.

I plop down next to my mom on the cozy couch, putting my purse on the coffee table and removing my sandals. I pick up my spirit notebook from the end table and flip through the pages. I should write down today's events, but I'm too tired to relive the drama.

"It's unprostitutional!" my mom says, shouting at the television. Tiger Woods and his hos have been all over the news for months and personally, I'm tired of the shit. If his wife wants to deal with his trifling behavior, why do I care what he does?

"Mom, is that even a word?" I ask, flipping through my spirit notes and trying to concentrate. I have a lot of work to catch up on, not to mention the personal things I want to focus on, even if I can't think straight. But with my mom here yelling at the television and sitting on my bed, I doubt I'll get to sleep anytime soon.

"It is if I say it is," my mom says, reaching for the pretty gift basket my cousin Jay gave her for Mother's Day and pulling out a bottle of lotion. I feel for him not having either of his parents around. Even if Jay's mom did call earlier, it's rare for her to talk to Jay, or Mama for that matter. Mama's always silent about what happened between her and her younger daughter, but I know she thinks about her a lot and so does Jay.

"So how long do you plan on hiding the truth from Mama?" my mom asks during a commercial break from her gossip news show. Her gift sure does smell good. I wonder if she'll share.

"As long as I can. You know she's going to make me give the powers back, you can even do such a thing." Stripping them away is more like it. Mama doesn't believe in me having more than my fair share of powers right now, limited to my dreams.

"You know it's not going to work for long, Jayd. The only reason she hasn't detected them yet is because she's so distracted with her initiations and stupid sons. You know she does a ritual to keep other people's madness out of her head while she's involved in the process, but as soon as she takes a break, she's going to hone in on your new development, and when she does, God help you." Why does my mom always have to be so theatrical with her shit?

I reach for the large gold basket on the table and claim a small bottle of lemon oil to sample. All the products look and smell delicious. Jay gave Mama the same thing, plus flowers and a card. He sure can pick a nice gift.

"Mom, you worry too much. Like I said, I'll keep your sight in my head for as long as I can. Once I master it, Mama will be so proud of me she'll have to let me hold on to your reclaimed powers," I say, massaging my hands and feet with the intoxicating liquid. I know Mama and Netta have the baddest beauty line available and my novice products aren't far behind theirs, but it's nice to try something different.

"Are we talking about the same Mama?" my mom asks, snatching the bottle away from me. "Mama doesn't have to do a damn thing. You know it and I know it. Hell, the whole damn world knows it, Jayd." My mom rises from the couch and walks toward her bedroom. "You're playing with fire, little girl, hiding this from your grandmother. She's not going to be happy at all when she finds out you've been sitting on this for so long." I get up from my comfy spot and follow her.

"I know, Mom. It'll be okay—you'll see," I say, claiming a corner at the foot of her queen-sized bed. I wish I felt comfortable sleeping in her room when she's gone, but I'd rather be in the living room in case someone tries to break in. That way I can hear them walk up the stairs, and prepare myself ahead of time.

"I wish I could say the same thing for you, little one, but I can't." My mom looks at me, worried that I've bitten off more than I can chew. "Jayd, how come you didn't tell me about you retaining this power from one of your dreams, especially since the sight you now possess once belonged to me?" I watch my mom sit down on her bed, and now I realize I've hurt her feelings. I didn't even know that was possible. She's usually so hard core. My mom looks at me, her emerald eyes tearing up. Now I really feel bad.

"Mom, I just didn't think you were interested."

"Jayd, if it has anything to do with my baby, I'm interested. And besides, you can look in that book all you want. It's still not better than firsthand information when you can get it." I never thought about it like that. My mom's got a good point, especially since there's limited information in the spirit book about my mom's path because she stopped keeping up with her notes in high school. I jog back into the living room, retrieve my notebook and pen, and again make myself comfortable on her bed.

"Okay, what you got?" I ask, happy for the night tutorial session. I can sleep after she's gone.

"Memories and regret." That's the first time I've ever heard my mom express regret about anything short of marrying my dad.

Exactly, she says in my mind. *Had I not been so hotheaded in the first place, I would still have my powers, and I was just getting good at them, too,* my mom continues, eyeing the disheveled room around her. When she left my dad seventeen years ago, she also left the house and everything in it.

"I'll help you keep my sight under one condition, Jayd.

The next time you need help, ask. The last thing I want you to do is have a meltdown like I did."

"It's a deal," I say, smiling at my mom. She can be real sweet when she wants to be. But like Mama, me, and the rest of the women in our lineage, cross us and nice turns to nasty real quick. My uncle Kurtis is learning that lesson the hard way now.

"And you have to tell Mama," my mom adds. "Now that I know, I'm an accomplice and I can't lie to Mama about this. Promise me that you'll tell her, Jayd."

"That's two things," I say, watching my mom get comfortable in her bed that she rarely uses. She pulls back the black and gold comforter, revealing gold satin sheets, and slides her dainty feet underneath.

"They go together, Jayd. And telling Mama sooner rather than later is of the utmost importance. Mama's got all kinds of tricks up her sleeve that you know nothing about. I hope you never have to find out what happens when one of her daughters crosses her."

"I know, right. I'd hate to be Uncle Kurtis right now," I say, getting under the oversized blanket from the opposite end of the bed.

"Mama can be as sweet as honey and as lethal as a rattlesnake when she wants to be. Listen to what I'm telling you, girl," my mom says, fluffing a large pillow behind her head. "Don't push Mama too far or she will hurt you. It may be out of love, but it'll still hurt."

"Okay, okay. I'll tell her," I say, reaching for the small accent pillows on the other side of the bed and propping myself up, ready to learn. "Now, tell me everything you can remember about your ability to chill a person's mind out. It's a dope power to have, Mom." My mom smiles at my enthusiasm and I'm glad to spend some time with her. Finally, she is choosing time with her daughter over her man, and I'm grateful for it.

"The first thing you need to learn is that everything has side effects, Jayd. Read the label carefully, which in our case is the spirit book. When you retained my vision from your dream, you should have looked for stories about things that happened to me after I started using my powers, not just the ways I used them. For example, the night I almost killed your father with my eyes when I tapped into his mind, witnessing his premarital infidelity firsthand," my mom says, as cool as ice. "I scared myself I was so angry, and my powers almost got away from me."

"You never told me about that," I say, writing as fast as I can. I should've got a tape recorder for this lesson.

"Because you never asked. You should be much further along in your studies by now, Jayd. Even I know that." She sounds just like Mama and Netta. I know I'm not on my game if my mom agrees with them. My mom and Netta have a tense relationship, but it's improved over time.

"But you know what a full plate I have, Mom. With cheer practice, the spring play, the debutante ball and being president of the African Student Union, I haven't had much time to study."

"Like I said, everything has side effects." My mom's right. Luckily the cotillion and the play are temporary. I'll have to find a better way to juggle the rest of my activities. My spirit work can't remain the primary sacrifice.

"The second thing you need to know is that cold things tend to be slippery, which can be both good and bad. When you want to easily access someone's mind and cool his or her thoughts immediately, it's a very good thing. But when the mind is too hot, it can tend to cause your cool to boil, causing a mental meltdown of sorts, and that can be very dangerous," my mom says, pulling the comforter tighter. "I've literally almost drowned in someone else's negative thoughts before. I don't wish that feeling on anyone," my mom says, shuddering at the memory. I'm shaking, and I don't even know what she went through, nor do I want to.

"Is that why women in our lineage are afraid of water?" I say, continuing my note taking.

"Partially, and also because we have a healthy respect for nature's power to build and destroy. Any type of drowning isn't fun."

"I hear that." I took swim lessons at the YMCA when I was ten years old and nearly drowned. Lifeguard or not, you won't catch my ass in deep water again.

"Those two lessons will go a long way when deciding whose thoughts to probe. Be careful who and when you try to help because as with Mickey's labor, the experience can turn on you like a pit bull. If you had known then what you know now, you would've never jumped into your friend's mind when you did." My mom's right. I have a lot to learn about her powers and my own. And with a few more sessions like this one between me and my mom, a sistah will be back on her A game in no time, good sleep included.

My mom left late last night after we stayed up talking most of the time away. I fell asleep soon after and am grateful for the dreamless rest. I never did get to wash my hair last night, so I woke up early this morning to get a quick wash and blow-dry in before my school day begins.

I turn the hot-water knob and then the middle one to full blast, welcoming the steam. Showers wake me up every morning.

I step into the shower, closing the sliding glass doors. After bathing, I lather the shampoo, scrubbing my scalp good before massaging it through my hair. It always feels good getting a clean start in the morning. Rubbing the mango-scented lather into my tresses, my fingers suddenly feel like jelly and my head, cold. Am I dreaming? My fingers continue moving up my hair until I can no longer feel anything. Instead, my hair is feeling me.

"Aaah!" I scream, opening my eyes, allowing the soap and water on my face to cloud my vision. The fingers in my hair continue to walk their way down my scalp and around my neck, stifling my sound. Without the use of my hands, I'm defenseless against my strangler. If this were a dream I would try to wake up, or at least have Mama somewhere around to help me. But I'm wide awake experiencing this nightmare, and alone.

Water, Jayd. Use the water to rinse your eyes, my mom says into my mind with panic in her voice. This shit feels too real to be a regular vision.

Near fainting, I turn around and rinse my face off in the water. The feeling slowly returns to my hands. I push my hair back and feel around my neck to loosen the ghostly grip, but I can't. The steam seeps up my nostrils, clearing my airways and melting the fingers around my neck.

That's it, Jayd. Inhale and then exhale. It's not real, baby. Mind over matter, my mom says, helping to calm my nerves. Finally free, I reach for the metal knobs to turn off the water to end this nightmare on Larch Street, but not before I lose my footing and fall flat on my ass, hitting my head on the back of the ceramic tub.

"Ouch!" I say, rubbing my head in the same spot where I hit it falling on black ice in one of my dreams. It's already tender from that experience and now I've reopened that wound. What the hell is really going on?

It's like I told you last night, Jayd. You're holding on to the residual negative emotions from your clients. You have to get rid of it before it drives you crazy, and Mama's the only one who can tell you exactly what to do. I hate it when my mom's right and I'm suffering the consequences in the midst of her revelation. *You have to tell Mama, Jayd. Now get yourself up and shake it off or you're going to be late for school.*

"Can a sistah get a little sympathy?" I ask aloud, picking myself up and grabbing the towel from the back of the shower door to dry off. I guess I'll be wearing my hair wet today with some leave-in conditioner since my shower was cut short.

Hell no, you can't get any sympathy. You asked for it and here it is. I know it sounds mean, Jayd, but I'm telling you the truth. There's so much more to our visions you don't know, and that ignorance alone can harm you. Tell Mama today. 'Bye, my mom says, checking out and leaving me to my Monday.

I'll tell Mama about this one as soon as possible, but I have to get through the rest of the school day first. I'll see Mama at Netta's shop when I go to work this afternoon. Until then, I'll have to deal with this madness on my own.

START YOUR OWN BOOK CLUB

Courtesy of the DRAMA HIGH series

ABOUT THIS GUIDE

The following is intended to help you get
the book club you've always wanted
up and running!
Enjoy!

Start Your Own Book Club

A Book Club is not only a great way to make friends, but it is also a fun and safe environment for you to express your views and opinions on everything from fashion to teen pregnancy. A Teen Book Club can also become a forum or venue to air grievances and plan remedies for problems.

The People

To start, all you need is yourself and at least one other person. There's no criteria for who this person or persons should be other than their having a desire to read and a commitment to discuss things during a certain time frame.

The Rules

Just as in Jayd's life, sometimes even Book Club discussions can be filled with much drama. People tend to disagree with each other, cut each other off when speaking, and take criticism personally. So, there should be some ground rules:

1. Do not attack people for their ideas or opinions.
2. When you disagree with a Book Club member on a point, disagree respectfully. This means that you do not denigrate other people or their ideas, i.e., no name-calling or saying, "That's stupid!" Instead, say, "I can respect your position; however, I feel differently."
3. Back up your opinions with concrete evidence, either from the book in question or life in general.
4. Allow everyone a turn to comment.
5. Do not cut a member off when the person is speaking. Respectfully wait your turn.
6. Critique only the idea. Do not criticize the person.

7. Every member must agree to and abide by the ground
   rules.

Feel free to add any other ground rules you think might be
necessary.

The Meeting Place

Once you've decided on members, and agreed to the ground
rules, you should decide on a place to meet. This could be
the local library, the school library, your favorite restaurant, a
bookstore, or a member's home. Remember, though, if you
decide to hold your sessions at a member's home, the location should rotate to another member's home for the next
session. It's also polite for guests to bring treats when attending a Book Club meeting at a member's home. If you choose
to hold your meetings in a public place, always remember
to ask the permission of the librarian or store manager. If you
decide to hold your meetings in a local bookstore, ask the
manager to post a flyer in the window announcing the Book
Club to attract more members if you so desire.

Timing Is Everything

Teenagers of today are all much busier than teenagers of the
past. You're probably thinking, "Between chorus rehearsals,
the Drama Club, and oh yeah, my job, when will I ever have
time to read another book that doesn't feature Romeo and
Juliet!" Well, there's always time, if it's time well-planned and
time planned ahead. You and your Book Club can decide to
meet as often or as little as is appropriate for your bustling
schedules. *Once a month* is a favorite option. *Sleepover Book
Club* meetings—if you're open to excluding one gender—is
also a favorite option. And in this day of high-tech, savvy teens,
Internet Discussion Groups are also an appealing option. Just
choose what's right for you!

Well, you've got the people, the ground rules, the place, and the time. All you need now is a book!

The Book

Choosing a book is the most fun. PUSHIN' is of course an excellent choice, and since it's part of a series, you won't soon run out of books to read and discuss. Your Book Club can also have comparative discussions as you compare the first book, THE FIGHT, to the second, SECOND CHANCE, and so on.

But depending upon your reading appetite, you may want to veer outside of the Drama High series. That's okay. There are plenty of options, many of which you will be able to find under the Dafina Books for Young Readers Program in the coming months.

But don't be afraid to mix it up. Nonfiction is just as good as fiction and a fun way to learn about from where we came without just using a history textbook. Science fiction and fantasy can be fun, too!

And always, always research the author. You might find that the author has a Web site where you can post your Book Club's questions or comments. The author may even have an e-mail address available so you can correspond directly. Authors might also sit in on your Book Club meetings, either in person, or on the phone, and this can be a fun way to discuss the book as well!

The Discussion

Every good Book Club discussion starts with questions. PUSHIN', as does every book in the Drama High series, comes with a Reading Group Guide for your convenience, though of course, it's fine to make up your own. Here are some sample questions to get started:

1. What's this book all about anyway?
2. Who are the characters? Do we like them? Do they remind us of real people?
3. Was the story interesting? Were real issues that are of concern to you examined?
4. Were there details that didn't quite work for you or ring true?
5. Did the author create a believable environment—one that you could visualize?
6. Was the ending satisfying?
7. Would you read another book from this author?

Record Keeper

It's generally a good idea to have someone keep track of the books you read. Often libraries and schools will hold reading drives where you're rewarded for having read a certain number of books in a certain time period. Perhaps a pizza party awaits!

Get Your Teachers and Parents Involved

Teachers and parents love it when kids get together and read. So involve your teachers and parents. Your Book Club may read a particular book whereby it would help to have an adult's perspective as part of the discussion. Teachers may also be able to include what you're doing as a Book Club in the classroom curriculum. That way, books you love to read, such as the Drama High ones, can find a place in your classroom alongside the books you don't love to read so much.

Resources

To find some new favorite writers, check out the following
resources. Happy reading!

Young Adult Library Services Association
http://www.ala.org/ala/yalsa/yalsa.htm

Carnegie Library of Pittsburgh
Hip-Hop!
Teen Rap Titles
http://www.carnegielibrary.org/teens/books

TeensPoint.org
What Teens Are Reading
http://teens.librarypoint.org/reading_matters

Teenreads.com
http://www.teenreads.com

Book Divas
http://www.bookdivas.com

Meg Cabot Book Club
http://www.megcabotbookclub.com

HAVEN'T HAD ENOUGH? CHECK OUT THESE GREAT SERIES FROM DAFINA BOOKS!

DRAMA HIGH

by L. Divine

Follow the adventures of a young sistah who's learning that life in the hood is nothing compared to life in high school.

THE FIGHT	SECOND CHANCE	JAYD'S LEGACY
ISBN: 0-7582-1633-5	ISBN: 0-7582-1635-1	ISBN: 0-7582-1637-8
FRENEMIES	LADY J	COURTIN' JAYD
ISBN: 0-7582-2532-6	ISBN: 0-7582-2534-2	ISBN: 0-7582-2536-9
HUSTLIN'	KEEP IT MOVIN'	HOLIDAZE
ISBN: 0-7582-3105-9	ISBN: 0-7582-3107-5	ISBN: 0-7582-3109-1
CULTURE CLASH	COLD AS ICE	
ISBN: 0-7582-3111-3	ISBN: 0-7582-3113-X	

BOY SHOPPING

by Nia Stephens

An exciting "you pick the ending" series that lets the reader pick Mr. Right.

BOY SHOPPING	LIKE THIS AND LIKE THAT	GET MORE
ISBN: 0-7582-1929-6	ISBN: 0-7582-1931-8	ISBN:0-7582-1933-4

DEL RIO BAY

by Paula Chase

A wickedly funny series that explores friendship, betrayal, and how far some people will go for popularity.

SO NOT THE DRAMA	DON'T GET IT TWISTED	THAT'S WHAT'S UP!
ISBN: 0-7582-1859-1	ISBN: 0-7582-1861-3	ISBN: 0-7582-2582-2
WHO YOU WIT?	FLIPPING THE SCRIPT	
ISBN: 0-7582-2584-9	ISBN: 0-7582-2586-5	

PERRY SKKY JR.

by Stephanie Perry Moore

An inspirational series that follows the adventures of a high school football star as he balances faith and the temptations of teen life.

PRIME CHOICE	PRESSING HARD	PROBLEM SOLVED
ISBN: 0-7582-1863-X	ISBN: 0-7582-1872-9	ISBN: 0-7582-1874-5
PRAYED UP	PROMISE KEPT	
ISBN: 0-7582-2538-5	ISBN: 0-7582-2540-7	